Fifties Chix: Keeping Secrets

Angela Sage Larsen

Published by Premiere

For my amazing nieces: Kezzie, Tessa, Mackenzie and Isabelle; and for Kaleigh, Anna, Olivia, Jorie and Julia. My hope is for you to know how extraordinary you each truly are and how much you have to give.

❧

Check out www.FiftiesChix.com for updates on the Fifties Chix book series, more info on your fave characters, secret diary entries, quizzes, contests and more!

❧

Acknowledgments

Eternal thanks to my wonderful editor, Lori Van Houten and fabulous copy editor, Liz Wallingford. Grateful acknowledgment to my family for their ongoing enthusiasm, love and support. Michele Luper, there is no one I'd rather live next door to; when you move, we're going with you. Special thanks to the hardest working, kindest agent on the planet, Bruce Butterfield, and to the remarkably skilled and generous team at FastPencil Premiere. I'm especially grateful to Marie Stroughter for her insight, feedback, and expertise and for sharing the brilliant René with me! I'm honored to once again have the glorious artwork of Astrid Sheckels gracing the interior of this book. And as always, I am happily and willingly indebted to my partner in life and business, my exceptional husband, Whit.

Contents

1

Now What?

Her hand was shaking so badly, she couldn't open her locker. She hadn't slept in two nights, and now, even more than before, she wondered if her whole life had dissolved into one everlasting hallucination. Looking down at her saddle shoes, she noticed an untied shoelace and scuffed toes. Just weeks ago, she would have died before wearing shoes with scuffs. But in this moment, it was like she hovered somewhere outside herself, looking down on her vacant body.

Mary Donovan was lost, furious, and frankly, *hurt*.

And it was all her social studies teacher's fault.

"I don't understand what's happening," Judy White whimpered at lunch. Beverly Jenkins and Ann Branislav, who had in the last couple of weeks become two of her four best friends, huddled around the table with her.

Beverly, usually the most easy-going of the five of them, was irritable today, finding Judy's characteristic naïveté vexing. "Don't go ape," Bev sighed impatiently.

Across the table, Ann looked distracted. She wore a light blue twin sweater set in the middle of May, but couldn't stop shivering. She pulled her sweater closer around her. She glanced around the school cafeteria to catch a glimpse of her not-so-secret crush. It felt funny to look for James O'Grady, or even just to think of him at all, when everything seemed to be falling apart. But wasn't that just when you wanted a sweetheart, when you needed someone to tell you it's not so bad? Only how could he be her sweetheart when she barely knew him? Worse, when she didn't even know who – or when – she herself was? After the dance Saturday night, she'd felt like she was slogging through quicksand, just trying to keep her head from going under. Just when she had started to find some peace, it had all slipped away from her grasp.

"This is all Miss Boggs's fault, isn't it?" asked Judy.

"Her name is Mrs. Fairview now," Bev corrected, not answering Judy's question. Before their conversation could continue, they were interrupted. Two girls who used to play on Bev's softball team before she had moved on to play for the boys' baseball team approached their table. Their centerpiece, Bev's nemesis, bad news Diane Dunkelman, was noticeably absent.

"Hey, Bev," said one. She sounded sincere enough. "Sweet game Saturday."

"Gee, thanks," Bev answered, mystified. Only last week, the girls had been following Diane around like she was the heppest girl on Earth. As they gave a friendly wave and turned to go, Bev and Ann couldn't help but notice that one of the girls was wearing a scarf around a ponytail and the other was wearing – *could that be right?* – cat-eye glasses.

The popular girls' visit to their table was enough to divert Judy's attention, although she hadn't noticed the details of their accessories.

"Golly, why do you think they came to say hi?" she wondered.

"I haven't the foggiest," Bev muttered. One more mystery was the last thing she wanted. As if waking up fifty-five years into the future, being drafted to pitch baseball for the boys' team, and liking a boy her parents wouldn't approve of weren't enough, now she had to figure out why her arch-rival's flunkies were starting to dress like her and her friends. Oh, and she had just found out that as far as she could tell, all their problems were thanks to a school project about the future. Her whole life had been turned upside down for a kooky teacher and a lousy grade. Just swell.

Maxine stared up at the picture of the President of the United States of America and chewed on the end of her pencil. Her history teacher's voice droning on at the front of the class was just background noise. Her mind was full and her heart felt divided. She thought of the essay about civil rights she had written for the school's underground paper, wondering when it would be published. She didn't know if she'd even be around for it; after all, just weeks ago, her life was totally normal in 1955 . . . well, as normal as it could be for a black girl going to a mostly white school only a year after *Brown v. Board of Education*. Today she was in a new century, surrounded by familiar faces, but amidst crazy circumstances, including a black President. She hadn't even decided yet if life was good in this parallel universe into which she had been thrust, when it suddenly became more complicated.

Her mind drifted, as it inevitably had during the last forty hours or so, to her social studies teacher, Miss Boggs. Maxine had been assigned a school project by Miss Boggs to predict life fifty-five years into the future. It might have been a cool enough assignment except that Maxine had had to do the assignment with four other girls, all of them white, all of them different from her. Even that hadn't turned out so bad. When it had gotten weirdsville was when the five of them had all woken up fifty-five years into the future they had been assigned to predict! Their families and friends were still there, but modern, and the only person missing was Miss Boggs.

Maxine swallowed hard when she thought through the next part. Saturday night at the school dance, the five of them had discovered quite by accident that Miss Boggs was not in fact missing, but that she had actually aged (when evidently no one else had); and she was still their social studies teacher, only now she went by her married name, Mrs. Fairview. When the girls had made this discovery, they had felt betrayed. After all, Mrs. Fairview must have had something to do with their predicament, they surmised: she had given the assignment and when the five girls shared a good-bye malt after they completed the project, Miss Boggs had mysteriously appeared and made them all promise to be friends in fifty-five years. Yet as they clearly struggled to fit into their new surroundings in the future, she hadn't stepped forward to help or offer any answers.

Out of all of them, Mary had taken it hardest. For reasons that were unclear to Maxine, she seemed to feel that she had a special connection to Miss Boggs, and she was frosted to discover that she had been kept out of orbit.

The five girls were counting down the hours and minutes to fifth period social studies, where they would confront Miss Boggs – er, Mrs. Fairview – themselves.

They had no idea what they would say, but they knew it had to be said.

Beverly, Maxine, Ann, and Judy sat in their usual huddle at the beginning of fifth period. They waited for Mary to arrive before the bell rang. They were each holding their breath, knowing how upset Mary would be when she discovered what they had upon entering class: a substitute teacher.

Sure enough, when Mary entered, she hadn't even looked their way but searched the front of the room for Mrs. Fairview. Her shoulders slumped and she looked like she was going to cry as her lip quivered. She made her way to her friends. Their pitying, sympathetic glances were not going to help her make it through class without falling apart.

"We'll find her, Mary," Judy encouraged. "We can use my . . . uh, *computer* to track her down. Maybe find her home address? We'll go after school." Judy knew that the computer was a sore subject with Mary. Mary liked to be in the know, but thanks to Judy's discovery of the computer at her house and her developing skill in using it, Mary was starting to feel left behind.

Now a tear trickled from out behind Mary's cat-eye glasses. She shook her head. "I have to pick up the baby after school."

"The baby?" Ann asked, confused. Perhaps Mary was referencing one of her three younger siblings.

"My project for home sciences, or whatever it's called. I have to take care of a machine baby."

"You mean a *computerized* –" Maxine started to correct Mary, but stopped cold when she saw the miserable look on Mary's face. Just then the bell rang to start class. They turned and faced front, and the substitute teacher, a man who looked like he was barely older than the students, introduced himself.

Maxine's cousin, Conrad Marshall, bounded in to class. A few kids gave out a "woot!" in honor of Conrad's performance in a couple of baseball games over the weekend. He was also returning after a three-day suspension for pulling the fire alarm as a prank.

"Sorry," he muttered to the sub for his tardiness, making his way to the back of the class. As he passed Bev, he gave her a little wink that made her stomach drop, her heart leap, and her mind whirl. She had faintly hoped that she could control this sort of thing and have a more casual response to his presence. After all, they had just played together on the boys' baseball team, winning two games to advance to the district championships. But her feelings for him only seemed to be getting stronger. She wished she could just take advantage of the strange and wonderful opportunity the future had provided for her to pitch for the varsity baseball team and focus on her athletics. But there was Conrad at the heart of every game and practice, at the heart of her favorite sport. He could not be avoided.

Mary raised her hand, interrupting the substitute's reading of the roll call and obligatory careful mispronunciation of each name.

"Yes?" He acknowledged her hesitantly.

"Where is Miss . . . er, *Mrs.* Fairview?"

"I don't know. They just called me to come in, so I came in." He gave her what was probably meant to be a charming smile, but Mary found it irritating.

"But how long will she be gone?"

Mr. Andrews, who told the class they could call him "Kip," sighed impatiently. "I don't know, Miss . . . ?"

"Miss Donovan, but *you* can call me *Mary*," she muttered with insolence.

Her four friends gasped and some of the other kids giggled. "Kip" reddened. If he didn't nip this in the bud, he'd never get the students' attention – or their respect.

"Is there something I can help you with, Mary?" He turned up the charm a notch, trying to sound a little more patient. He usually didn't have a problem garnering approval from students.

"I sincerely doubt it, *Kip*." Mary was surprised at the impertinent words that flew so easily out of her mouth, as if she were in the habit of talking back to authority figures.

After a beat wherein Kip couldn't decide how to respond to Mary in a clever way, he said, "Well, Mary, how would you like to take a little visit to the office? Maybe they could answer your questions and help you adjust your attitude."

"Fine." Mary stood up stiffly, trying to appear bold, but her friends could tell she was quaking ever so slightly. They'd never seen her be discourteous to an adult, never mind a *teacher*. She gathered up her books and walked with fake confidence out the door, her ponytail swinging a deceptively cheerful rhythm.

As the door closed behind her, she heard Mr. Andrews challenge, "Anyone else?"

As soon as she was beyond the window in the classroom door, Mary crumpled into sobbing. *You have got to get it together, Mary Jane Donovan,* she told herself. But her own thoughts were drowned out by tears. She made her way haltingly to the office, wondering what she was supposed to tell them. Of course, she had never before been called to the principal. Would they call her mom or Nana and make one of them come pick her up? Would she be suspended? And what about that blasted computer baby she was supposed to pick up after school? Her sobbing received new impulse. By the time she arrived at the office, she was hiccuping and her glasses were steamed over.

"I got sent to the office," she blathered to the group of three secretaries sitting in desks behind the tall countertop. Two gazed at her disinterestedly and one offered her a tissue and invited her to sit and wait for a counselor. Mary perked up just a tiny bit: a counselor didn't sound as extreme as the principal. Feeling the first ray of hope in days, she turned and noticed for the first time a line of kids sitting and standing along the back wall. She made her way to the one empty plastic molded chair against the wall and blew her nose. She started to take deep breaths to stay her weeping.

Another student walked in and up to the counter. "Hi, Ms. Steadman sent me to find out something about her whiteboard?"

Mary realized with alarm to whom the voice belonged. She tucked her head down, tightening into the smallest ball possible in her seat. Maybe her crush James O'Grady would come and go without even noticing her. There were plenty of other kids surrounding her. If he just kept facing forward . . . .

A loud hiccup escaped Mary's mouth. Her eyes widened with horror, but she kept her chin down.

"Mary? Is that you?"

2

Why, Baby, Why?

As Mary sat in the counselor's office, she was torn between getting out soon enough to see James before he headed back to class or hiding out in utter humiliation. It was the second time in less than a week that he'd seen her in tears. And not the delicate, lady-in-distress kind; the should-only-be-breaking-down-in-private messy kind. It was too much. James O'Grady was an intelligent fellow and certainly he'd be interested in an intelligent girl – happy, cute and put-together. And interesting. Like Ann Branislav, one of her best friends and a competitor for James's attention and affections.

The counselor, Mrs. Snyder, could see that Mary was distracted; although she'd never had occasion to meet with Mary before, it was obvious she was not your run-of-the-mill troublemaker, with her conservative old-fashioned clothes and funny cat-eye glasses.

"Is there something you'd like to talk about, Mary?" she asked the tear-stained student fidgeting in front of her. Mrs. Snyder was a little distracted herself. There was a line out her door and her desk was overflowing with paperwork. A good sign for Mary, who was hoping against hope the counselor would not call her mother or Nana. Mrs. Snyder seemed to have much bigger fish to fry.

Suddenly Mary's eyes lit up, as though she'd had a sudden epiphany. She crafted her words as carefully as she could. "My favorite teacher is Mrs. Fairview. And I just found out that she's retiring. But there are only a few weeks of school left and she didn't come in today . . . ." Mary swallowed. "I wanted to make sure she was OK. But I don't . . . know how to get a hold of her."

Mrs. Snyder agreed that Mrs. Fairview was a likable teacher. Many students adored her. "But you can understand that school policy prohibits us from giving out her home address. You could always email her."

"Email?" Mary's face clouded again. She had no idea how to email someone . . . or, for that matter, what email was.

"You just use her first initial and last name with the school's web address," Mrs. Snyder said in a tone that indicated Mary should know exactly what she meant and that she considered the case closed.

"Right," Mary said. After a pause, she added, "Would you mind writing that down for me, please?"

The counselor dug around on her desk for a scrap piece of paper, a folder slipping off and sending papers skittering across the small patch of floor. With a sigh, she ignored the mess and jotted down a line of words, then passed it to Mary. Before Mary left, Mrs. Snyder dutifully advised her to be more respectful and to come back and talk whenever she needed to. Mary doubted

Mrs. Snyder would remember her if she came back in a half an hour asking for help.

As she exited the counselor's office with a quiet "Thank you," Mary tucked the note in her pocket, eager to get Judy or one of the other girls to help her figure out this email tool to contact Mrs. Fairview. James had left the office by that point and Mary felt the all-too-familiar mixed feeling of relief and disappointment.

After fifth period, to which Mary did not return, Judy, Ann, Maxine, and Bev met briefly in the hall. They spoke quickly because they needed to get to their next classes before the bell rang.

"What do we do?" Judy asked, hugging her books to her chest.

Bev said, "I have baseball practice after school, but maybe we should meet at Mary's house after that."

"Will she mind that?" Ann asked.

"I'm starting to worry about her," put in Maxine. "This whole thing has really rattled her cage. I think we should go to her pad and at least check in with her. We can go after Bev's practice like she said."

They promptly agreed and parted ways. A couple of girls whose names they didn't know strolled by and offered breezy hellos. One of the girls had rolled-up jeans and saddle shoes and the other wore a skirt very similar to the circle skirts Mary favored.

When the last bell of the day rang, Mary trudged with trepidation to her "home sciences" classroom. Her palms were sweaty. The last time her grade depended on a big assignment, the results had been a little more than she could handle. So she wasn't too keen on an assignment that included a computerized baby. Who knew what her life might be when she woke up tomorrow morning? She crossed herself before entering Mrs. Doss's classroom.

Many students had arrived before her, abuzz with excitement about the project. Obviously, they'd never woken up fifty-five years into the future like she had when she'd been assigned her "Travel to Tomorrow" project with Judy, Maxine, Ann, and Bev weeks ago in 1955. At the head of the classroom, Mrs. Doss stood with a few other adults, checking names off a list, handing out packets of info, collecting paperwork, and passing out ID bracelets, diaper bags, baby carriers, and bundles of mechanical joy.

Katie, a girl in Mary's class, rushed in behind Mary and asked if she was excited. Not waiting for an answer, Katie went on to gush about how she nearly forgot to get her permission slip signed. Mary groaned inwardly, *What is wrong with me? I have no signed permission slip!* She never would have been sent to the office, broken out in tears in public, spoken irreverently to an adult, or forgotten something for school in the past. What had happened to her resolve to treat her time-traveling dilemma like a Nancy Drew mystery? Nancy Drew would not have become a basket case like Mary had; Nancy Drew had moxie, determination, and grit. She was ladylike and smart and she was not intimidated by a challenge. It was time for Mary to pull herself up by the bootstraps and get something done, Nancy Drew-style. Starting with making this baby thing work.

And ending with finding Mrs. Fairview and getting some answers (including how to get back to 1955).

She managed to convince Mrs. Doss that she'd bring her permission slip to school tomorrow. Mary felt encouraged by this simple accomplishment because Mrs. Doss was initially not going to back down and let Mary proceed with the assignment without one. As soon as Mrs. Doss's assistant handed Mary the baby, however, Mary wondered why she had chosen this particular thing about which to be insistent. Before she even walked out of the classroom, the "infant" started fussing and crying. She turned back to Mrs. Doss, who just gave her a big smile and gestured toward the paperwork Mary had been handed that explained caring for the machinated rugrat.

Mary recalled a favorite saying of her Nana's . . . in years past, when one of Mary's sisters, twins Patty and Maggie, had wailed "Whyyyy?" when asked to do something, Nana would tell them there was no whining allowed and "why" was the beginning of "whine."

Mary jostled the baby gently and muttered, "Why, indeed?" and was surprised when the baby fell silent.

Maybe this could be OK, after all. Maybe it would even be fun.

Dear Diary,   17th of May

     I got sent to the office today at school! I don't even want to record that...maybe I'll burn this before I have children so that they will never know. Speaking of having kids, I had a baby today, too. A big day for Mary Jane Donovan!! So, to catch you up: did not get to see ~~Miss Boggs~~ Mrs. Fairview, instead substitute teacher was in, I mouthed off to him and got sent to the office, where I dissolved into tears, James O'Grady saw me sobbing like a fream, and then after school I retrieved a computerized baby for my Home Sciences class. That is my day in a nutshell. I should write an entry of what my day would have been in 1955:

"Dear Diary,

Today we made apple cobbler in Home Ec and I got an A! I bumped into James O'Grady on my way to English. Maybe tomorrow he'll say hi! I miss my father, but he's gone, so I just won't think about it until he comes around for Christmas. I'm going to make a cotton circle skirt for summer, just a few more weeks until summer vacation and Nana teaches me to drive!"

How simple my life was and I never even knew it. And now that tot from you-know-where is screaming at me and someone is at the door. I suppose I should go see who's here . . . and read the directions for that "baby" before I mess anything else up.

   Always,
    Mary

P.S. I'm going to start wearing the apron I made around...this "baby" does everything. And I mean everything...so I have diapers to change all hours of the day and night!

P.P.S. I have to write a diary just for keeping the baby. At least that won't be a stretch for me.

P.P.P.S. Maggie or Patty: STOP READING MY DIARY!

Poor Mary has gone round the bend. I still remember eyeballing her in social studies so long ago and thinking she had her act together. She makes all her clothes, always knows the answers and seemed so confident about who she is. She'd actually be pretty beat if she wasn't so square. But the other girls and I went to her house today . . . and she is not the same girl. Everything is upside down. According to my history class today, this has all the signs of a revolution: unrest, confusion, a call to progress. I don't know what the call to progress is, actually. I just know that when you're at rock bottom, you have nowhere to go but up.

Maxine

Dear Diary,   May 17

Today we had a substitute teacher in social studies - no Mrs. Fairview! Boy, was Mary frosted. She even got smart with the sub, Kip (that's his first name. He said we could call him by his first name! He's cute. How could he not be with a name like Kip? I can't believe I'm writing about another man. I'm so sorry, Bob!). Anyway, Mary got sent to the principal and she didn't even come back!! We went to see her after school. It's like when someone's sick, you take them their homework and maybe some cookies. Only we didn't bring cookies. And maybe Mary's not sick, but she's not herself! I think she was happy to see us, though. Us being the Fifties Chix (that's what the kids at school keep calling us, and I like it). She was surprised, but I think it made her happy. She reminds me of James Dean, a rebel without a cause. Except her cause is getting us back to 1955 by finding Mrs. Fairview, so that makes her a rebel with a cause! Also, her house is sure loud compared to mine. What a zoo. She's got those ankle-biter brother and sisters who don't sit still for a minute and on top of it, she had that crying baby that no one knows how to take care of. I mean, if it was a real baby, you could warm up some milk or something. I really thought Mary would be a great mom someday, but that was in another place and time. Oh, don't get me wrong. I still think she'll be a great mom...just not to a machine!! We couldn't stay for long, but we decided we are going to find Mrs. Fairview's house if she still isn't at school tomorrow and we'll go talk to her ourselves!
Didn't see Bob today. But on Weds. I am going to watch Bev's baseball practice (I already asked) and I'll see him there.
Judy

Conrad winked at me. How will I concentrate in a big game
with him in it if that's all I can remember about my whole
day??
OK, some other things about my day. No word on this whole
Travel to Tomorrow thing. Some of the kids at school are
wearing threads from the 1950s. My friend Mary's gone
ape.
And Conrad winked at me.
-Bev

Dearest Irina,   *17 May*
My sweetest cousin, how I wish you were here; or
I was there. Or we were together somewhere else!
It's not that I want to leave my friends, but I
wouldn't mind a break from this chaos! We just
feel like we are getting the royal shaft. Someday
I'll explain it all to you. In the meantime, keep me
distracted. Tell me about your American soldier
there in Belgrade.
∂—Ann

3

Like Clockwork

Mary stood in front of Mrs. Doss's desk in third period home sciences, bleary-eyed and comatose.

"I don't have my permission slip signed, so I'm returning the baby." She held out the eight-pound bundle, which was not so much bundled as loosely shoved in a thin blanket. For effect, and to perfectly complement Mary's bloodshot eyes, the baby emitted a high steady howl.

Mrs. Doss was unmoved. She smiled and said, "It's true that you need a permission slip, but I have the feeling you're trying to get out of this assignment, Mary."

"Maybe I am, but I have too many other things going on right now. I can't do this on top of it all!"

"See, you are already getting the point! The assignment is working. It's hard to raise a baby as a teenage mother out of wedlock; it *is* hard to balance everything. But I know you're up for it. Of all my students, I have faith in you. Now read your directions and bring your slip tomorrow." Mrs. Doss took the baby from Mary, properly swaddling it in the blanket, then handed it back to Mary with such tenderness, you would have thought it was a real baby. The crying stopped.

Mary sighed in relief for that one simple grace and returned to her desk, Mrs. Doss's words about being a teenage mom sinking in. *Was that something that should be discussed out loud?* In a strange mental leap, Mary recalled a classmate she knew of in 1954 named Sherri who had had a serious romance with a football player. Sherri had suddenly gotten very sick and had to go live with relatives out of state. Sherri had come back the next year, her absence never spoken of, but now Mary wondered if the girl wasn't sick so much as a mother too soon. Mary felt stunned at Mrs. Doss's words, her own realization about Sherri Stapleton, and the overwhelming task Mary had been given in trying to balance all this in a strange new world. Mary couldn't wait to tell the other girls what she had concluded about their classmate and how shocking the premise of this "baby" project really was.

She steadied herself and took a deep breath, feeling somewhat better as she looked around the classroom and noticed the other kids with bags under their eyes and shell-shocked expressions. It made her long for her "old" class where all she had to do was roll out a crust for an apple pie, learn how to truss a turkey for the holidays, or sew a set of kitchen curtains.

The real fun would come when she had to attend all her other classes with a screeching tot in tow. Her least favorite activity was attracting unwanted attention. By the time fifth period arrived, she wasn't even excited to see the girls. She just wanted to go home and crawl in bed and leave her current school project in Nana's capable hands.

"Hiya!" Judy greeted Mary in her typical perky fashion.

Mary grumbled an unintelligible response. Maxine shot Ann a look that said Mary's sour disposition was getting old real fast. Bev, staring at the classroom door, seemed not to notice.

"How's it going?" Judy tried again.

Their substitute teacher, Kip, came in the classroom then, which made Mary pout and ignore Judy outright.

Maxine was about to speak up and defend Judy from Mary's maltreatment, but the bell rang. It was fine; they had agreed to find Mrs. Fairview today anyway and that was bound to help the situation – maybe they'd get some answers and their old Mary back.

After class, before Mary could rush off to P.E., Judy told her that she had found what she believed to be Mrs. Fairview's home address.

Instantly, Judy was back on Mary's radar screen. "Really, Judy?" Mary brightened perceptibly. "Gee, you're the most! Let's all meet after school and go to her house."

Judy grinned and nodded.

Mary had a hard time focusing on volleyball in P.E. (but this time not only because she abhorred physical education). She fantasized about seeing Mrs. Fairview again and she reveled in advance at her own magnanimous nature: she would forgive Mrs. Fairview's desertion of her (and her friends, of course) and offer her the chance to make it up to them. Mary's heart beat a little faster . . . maybe they would even find the answer they needed to go back to 1955! Maybe this was her last day in the future, her last day with this wretched mechanical infant, her last day with her father . . . . Wait, that didn't sound right. When she went back to 1955, she promised herself, she would be the family peacemaker and be sure to track down her dad and see him every week. And she'd get her act together and be perfectly charming and lovely to James; he would never see her cry again. She would be the picture of grace.

She felt positively on cloud nine at that moment. The moment right before she got beaned in the face with a volleyball and her nose spouted a fountain of blood.

Ann gasped at Mary's appearance. "What happened to you?"

Bev saw the embarrassed look on Mary's face and assured her, "It's not *that* bad."

"Spoken like a tomboy," Mary said, attempting wit. She still held a towel to her face, but the flow of blood had slowed down substantially.

The girls had met up at Mary's locker after school, where she was waiting for them with the baby on her hip and her head held in the air with gauze wadded against her nose.

"Do you need to go home?" Judy asked her, concerned.

"No!" Mary rushed to say. "No, I told the nurse not to call my mother or Nana. I want to see Mrs. Fairview."

The girls looked doubtful, but they understood where Mary was coming from. Frankly, none of them wanted to put off their visit either, and they knew it wasn't an option to go without Mary.

"Think I can leave this thing in my locker 'til tomorrow morning?" Mary asked, gesturing toward the baby.

Maxine laughed. Maybe getting her clock cleaned had knocked something loose in Mary's mood; her sense of humor, though dark, had at least improved.

"It's over two miles' walk," Judy said, pulling out a paper she'd printed out with a map to Mrs. Fairview's house. "Are you sure you're up to it?"

"Oh, golly, yes," Mary assured all of them. "Besides, whoever of the four of you isn't babysitting *this thing* can babysit me."

They giggled and went on their way, Bev taking the baby carrier and most of their books so she could fit in a little extra exercise and Ann cradling the baby, who appeared to be sleeping peacefully for once. As they walked, it was evident that it wasn't just Mary's mood that had recovered; they were all feeling a little more lighthearted and hopeful at the prospect of seeing their teacher.

Judy had found a few options for an address for "Fairview" in her search, including a "Mr. and Mrs. Reginald Fairview," but it was way across town, and so she hoped that the "M. Fairview" only a couple miles away was the one they were looking for.

As they walked, Judy mused, "You know, I don't know much about being a mother, and I definitely don't know anything about taking care of a computerized baby, but maybe calling it something other than 'This Thing' would help."

"Yes, Mary. Is your baby a boy or a girl?" Ann put in, glancing down at the lifelike doll in her arms.

"If you're asking if it's anatomically correct, the answer is yes. And it's a girl," Mary said, bringing her head level and testing for any remaining blood. Her nose throbbed, but at least it was drying up.

"*She's* a girl," Judy, who carried the diaper bag, corrected.

"What's *her* name?" Maxine asked.

"Grace," Mary said, deciding on the spot. She repeated it. "*Grace.*"

"That's lovely," Ann said.

As they continued to push on, following Judy's directions, Mary explained the baby project to them, but decided not to mention her theory about Sherri Stapleton after all. It felt too gossipy, and besides there were enough details about the baby project itself to entertain them. She explained, for example, that the baby came equipped with a computer that kept track of how often the baby cried or needed to be fed, rocked, changed, or burped; how quickly Mary responded; and whether or not she had done each task properly. She explained that you even had to carry the baby to support its neck or the computer would take note of it and make the baby cry. Ann had already figured this out as she propped the baby's head in the crook of her arm.

Mary showed them her bracelet. "This somehow links to the baby so the baby – Grace – knows I'm her mom." Mary added that there was a rumor in the class that their teacher, Mrs. Doss, could program the babies to be easygoing or cranky.

The girls marveled. "We sure didn't include all this in our Travel to Tomorrow project for Miss Boggs!"

As if deciding their peaceful musings had gone on long enough, "Grace" stirred and let out a shriek. "I think I got the cranky one," Mary murmured, taking the baby from Ann.

"Her house is on the next block," Judy said, consulting her directions. They walked the remainder of the way to their social studies teacher's house without talking, each involved in her own thoughts, with Grace's fussing as background music.

Maxine wondered if this was the beginning of the end of a very long, strange dream. Was the whole experience, in fact, some cosmic test? Had her writing the essay and courageously handing it to James O'Grady to be published been her accepting the challenge and prevailing? Was it the key to the puzzle that would enable her to return to 1955 all the wiser? Somehow it didn't quite all fit. For starters, the essay hadn't been actually published yet . . . .

Judy shifted the diaper bag to her other shoulder and thought of her friends. If this was the last day that they spent together in the future, if in fact Mrs. Fairview had had a hand in their time travel and would help them get back when they found her, Judy already felt a little homesick for it. She hoped, of course, that she would stay friends with the Fifties Chix (forever, like she had promised Miss Boggs), but it would be different back in 1955. No baseball for Bev, no black President for Maxine. There would still be Bob, certainly. That was a comfort. But there would probably also be that terrible Diane Dunkelman, leeching onto Bob and diverting his attention from Judy. *Would there be a dreamy Kip Andrews?* she wondered and then blushed, as if she had spoken it out loud.

Ann gazed around at the light filtering through the trees, making patterns on the sidewalk in front of her. Amazing how she could glide right through the little shadows untouched, how the color of her sweater, skin, shoes could darken so easily and then wash clean, unstained, with the next swatch of sunlight. How she wished she could pass through life like everything unpleasant was just a shadow, not leaving a mark. But her life, and the lives of those she loved, seemed irreparably stained by war and confusion. Her thoughts drifted to Anne Frank, as they often did ever since the first time Ann had read the girl's diary when it was published in 1952. After reading it over and over for nearly two solid years, Ann had finally tucked the book in the bottom of one of her dresser drawers in an attempt to live her own life. She felt like she could have *been* Anne Frank and that Anne Frank was a part of her, a part of her cousin Irina, and a part of all the relatives who had been killed by the same Nazis who had cut short Anne Frank's promising life.

She had become obsessed with Anne Frank's death and was still needing to become more "obsessed" with her own living (hence the book's new resting place in the drawer). James had become a sweet diversion. Ann's heart went out to him and his parents' divorce; she knew the pain of family trauma, of course, having lost her grandparents before she was even born and being constantly conscious of their absence. Though her parents were still married, sometimes she felt lonely even when among people she loved. She resolved to find a way to wash the pain off like the sun washed off the darkness. Could Mrs. Fairview help her do that and live a life that Anne Frank and millions of others had never had the chance to do?

With each step toward Mrs. Fairview's house, Bev's feet felt more and more like concrete. She wanted to turn and run the other way. If this visit to Mrs. Fairview meant the end of playing baseball, the end of being with Conrad, even if only as a teammate, she couldn't bear the thought. Sure, it would be nice to be back in good old predictable 1955 where she would be greeted by her mom every day after softball practice with a snack and she could enjoy family dinners again every night. But she just wasn't ready to give up this life quite yet. She knew the girls would be disappointed in her, in how selfish she was being. But she couldn't help it. Conrad had winked at her. And no one seemed to mind when they spoke to each other in public. A white girl and a black boy; no one even glanced twice!

They paused when Judy stopped. Following her gaze, they stared up at the towering Victorian brick house with ornate gingerbread details, all painted different autumnal colors. The yard was immaculate, shrubs trimmed back but on the verge of exploding into color at any moment. Several ancient maple trees seemed to pin the lawn down and anchor the property, which was bordered by a pristine white picket fence, as if it had been transported from another time and place and would take up and leave given the choice had it not been fastened down.

Compared to the houses around it, the estate did look out of place. The other homes had been either remodeled or rebuilt in modern suburban style and looked like they were in a hurry to get on with it, whereas this manor was dawdling in another century and really didn't care what everyone else was doing.

Mary had to smile. Somehow this seemed fitting for Mrs. Fairview's house.

Judy heaved a dramatic sigh. "Ready?"

The Fifties Chix looked at each other with ambivalent expressions. Instead of answering, they passed through the gate and moved down the path toward the door in, as they so often found themselves lately, one unit.

After ringing the doorbell, Mary was astonished, when the heavily-carved wooden door opened, to be once again face to face with James O'Grady.

4

Old Friends

"Mary! And . . . Ann . . . Maxine, and Bev . . . ." James couldn't help but laugh. His path kept inexplicably crossing with these girls and here they were on his doorstep. Including the little blonde who was always along for the ride, whom he was pretty sure was named Judy.

Ann and Mary were both stricken silent at the sight of their heartthrob, and Maxine and Bev scrutinized them for their reactions. It was "the little blonde" who spoke for all of them.

"Hiya. James, right? We may have the wrong house. We're looking for Miss B – er, Mrs. Fairview's house?"

"Oh, you got the right place. She's staying out back. But she's not home."

Ann and Mary continued to stare. James was in running shorts, a yellow T-shirt that had "Try Athlete" printed on it, and running shoes with thick soles. Referring to his wardrobe, he explained, "Track. I'm about to go out for a run."

"Where did she go, and when will she be back?" Bev had the presence of mind to ask, refocusing on the task at hand.

"Not sure on either count, honestly," James said. "She rents the apartment above my Aunt Row's garage." He gestured toward the back of the house with his thumb. "I just came by to help my aunt around the house. As you can tell, it's a lot for one little lady to take care of, but she doesn't want to give it up."

"Jimmy!" the girls heard an elderly voice chide from inside the house. But it sounded too cheerful to be scolding.

"Aunt Row, I'm not giving away any of your secrets, I promise!" James called over his shoulder to the voice. To the girls on the porch, he said, "I literally gotta run, but I can tell Aunt Row to give Mrs. F the message that you're looking for her."

Mary found her voice. "That would be swell."

It was then that he noticed she was rocking a fake baby and he chuckled again. "So, you have Mrs. Doss, do you? Lucky you."

"Yeah, lucky me," Mary agreed. Was it Ann's imagination, or were Mary's eyes literally sparkling? Ann felt a lump form at the base of her throat that made it hard to breathe.

They said their good-byes and James closed the door, joining them only momentarily on the wide wraparound porch before he jogged off down the street. Once again, Ann and Mary were mute. They gazed after him.

Judy corralled them away from the door toward the front gate, but Mary stopped them. "We can't leave now. We're no better off than before we came here . . . well, maybe a *little* better . . . well, I mean –" She stammered and blushed, causing Ann to cross her arms, roll her eyes, and emit a muffled sound that resembled, "Humph."

"We know what you mean, Mary," Maxine said. "But what do you recommend we do, pester the old lady inside?"

"I beg your pardon?" queried the voice of the old lady, who, it turned out, was no longer inside. She had poked her head through the front door and was surveying the group on her front lawn.

"Begging *your* pardon, ma'am," Maxine quickly atoned, bowing her head. "We were just . . . ." She drew a blank and the others all piped up at once:

"Mrs. Fairview has been missing from school!"

"We're looking for our teacher!"

"We've got to find Mrs. Fairview!"

"We're not trying to be nosy . . . ."

Aunt Row chuckled and her mannerisms reflected those of her nephew. "Oh, for goodness' sake. Don't just stand there babbling, come in for some tea."

Once inside, Aunt Row led the girls past a round parlor, which was the base of a three-story turret, and to the back of the house and a large sunny kitchen. There were knickknacks everywhere, and would have reminded Mary of her own house except that these trinkets looked like they each had an interesting story. The kitchen had a long counter dividing it from a breakfast area that had a wall of paned glass looking over the backyard. The countertop was a smooth, worn-with-use wood that gleamed in the sunlight flooding through the French doors and tall windows. Open shelves on every other wall where there weren't windows housed colorful bowls, pots, and glasses, all of them unique and mismatched. The effect was like an exotic marketplace specializing in one-of-a-kind vintage memorabilia. The scent of freshly baked bread, old wood, and something else sweet and unidentifiable filled their lungs as they breathed in the atmosphere and started to relax.

Aunt Row gestured for the girls to sit at an ancient pine-planked table that was probably at least ten feet long. Mary could see why James had to help Row take care of the place. It was more space than even a family of four or five would need. As Bev and Judy each pulled out a chair, two cats stretched, gave them dirty looks, and hopped down lazily, while another refused to acknowledge them or budge. Judy settled in awkwardly next to the kitty, taking less than half the seat.

Mary took a spot near the window and noticed the ivy-covered carriage house at the rear of the back garden. She could see four windows, all with window boxes of pansies and primroses. *That must be where Mrs. Fairview lives.* So odd to see that as her real home, as Mary was in the habit of imagining her living in a cottage or a big house instead.

Aunt Row took orders – tea with milk, ice water, and apple juice – and then put a slightly dinged copper kettle full of water on the stove. She came over to join the girls and disrupted yet another cat napping in a chair. "Oh, shoosh," she said, dismissing the ginger tabby's evil eye.

The girls watched her carefully. She had a kind of beauty from which it was hard to look away. Her snow white hair was in a bun constituted of smooth curls, and her pale skin was totally unlined, despite what the girls surmised her age must be. She had big laughing dark gray eyes and delicate features. She was cheerful and charming and didn't seem like the type of person who could live alone (of course, she didn't . . . there were cats multiplying by the moment). She wore no jewelry, had no wedding ring on her finger.

She asked for introductions without giving the girls funny looks for how they were dressed or for carting around a mechanical baby. The girls each said their names and asked politely what they should call their hostess.

"My name is Rowena, but everyone calls me Aunt Row, so I guess you should call me that."

Noticing Mary's bundle, Aunt Row asked the name of Mary's baby. Self-consciously, Mary told her, "Grace."

"Well, I'll be. That's Jimmy's mama's name."

Mary blushed involuntarily at the mention of James and his nickname and was pleased with the connection between "her baby" and James's mother.

Before the conversation went much further, Judy thought they should clarify an important point. "It's not a real baby. It's computerized; it's Mary's project for school."

"Will wonders never cease," declared Row, but she didn't sound surprised. In fact, she sounded like she had known all along. "Does May know about this? She would get a kick out of it."

"We . . . don't know. That's part of the reason we're here," Mary responded. "We're trying to find Mrs. Fairview. She hasn't been at school. And . . ." Mary paused.

Maxine came to the rescue. "And we have some questions for her."

"Oh, land. To hear May called 'Mrs. Fairview' still tickles me," sighed Aunt Row. She gazed out the window as if remembering another time and place.

The girls shifted uncomfortably in their seats. "When do you expect her back?" Judy asked.

"Lord knows. I'm not the girl's keeper. She is always coming and going and never tells me anything. I'm sure she'll be back soon."

The kettle began to rattle and whistle and Aunt Row excused herself.

"Can I help?" Maxine and Ann offered simultaneously.

Aunt Row smiled. "Well, aren't you polite? It's like you're from another era." She didn't seem to notice when the girls glanced at each other, wide-eyed. "Come on over and help me pour. Kettle's getting heavier every day."

Though Mary was feeling at ease in Aunt Row's kitchen – in fact, it was more at home than she'd felt in a long while – she was still keen to find out about Mrs. Fairview's return.

"Aunt Row, when you say she'll be back soon, do you mean today, or within a week, or a month?"

"Exactly, sweetheart. Oops, your Grace needs you."

Mary's baby had started crying. *Never a moment of peace,* Mary thought, tempted to try to find an inappropriate way to silence the mechanical papoose.

Ann and Maxine found teacups and glasses, following Aunt Row's directions while she filled up a tray with cookies, biscuits, and muffins. Ann asked where she was from. "I've lived a little bit of everywhere, but this has always been home. I grew up in this house. In fact, May Boggs and I used to play dollies right over there when we were girls." She pointed to a spot just past where Mary sat and Mary thought, *Playing dollies, just like I am right now.*

"Is 'May' a nickname for Marion?" Judy asked. In 1955, the girls' social studies teacher (who had given them their Travel to Tomorrow assignment) had been named May Boggs. When the girls had woken up inexplicably fifty-five years into the future, no one around them had aged. Miss Boggs had gone missing – or so they had thought, until it turned out that Marion Fairview was the one and the same Miss May Boggs; only she *had* aged, while no one else had. This got Mary to thinking . . . *if we were to go back to 1955, would we discover that Aunt Row was a young woman then, just like Miss Boggs?*

Answering Judy's question, Aunt Row said, "She's always been May to me; but when she married Reggie – Reginald – Fairview, she wanted to be Mrs. Marion – her given name – Fairview. Can you help me carry this tray, sweetheart?" she asked Ann. Maxine carried over a stack of mismatched porcelain dessert plates and a bouquet of assorted antique silver spoons.

"How long have you and Mrs. Fairview been friends, then?" Maxine asked the loaded question.

"Oh, my. Forever and a day," Aunt Row answered vaguely.

"When did she get married?" pressed Mary.

As Aunt Row searched her mind, Judy said without thinking, "It must not have been 1955." Aunt Row gave her a funny look and Judy quickly added, "Was it? Because that was the year my . . . grandparents got married." Her theatrical improvisation skills were proving useful. Or so she hoped.

"Hm. Not sure I'd remember, dear." Aunt Row's disposition seemed to shift suddenly. After a brief pause, she said, "Well, finish up your tea. I'm sure you girls have lots of homework. And Mary, I can see you have your hands full with your . . . project." She waved in the direction of Mary and the baby. The dismissal felt insulting compared to how she had been treating them all just seconds before.

"Can we help you clean up?" Bev asked after downing her apple juice in one gulp.

"No, thank you. Gives me something to do, and besides, that's what Jimmy's for."

The girls began to gather their things. "I'll tell Mrs. Fairview you came by," Aunt Row said, for the first time referencing her friend by something other than her first name.

Mary began to remind her of their names. "Yes, please. Tell her that Mary, Beverly –"

"I know, I know, and Jane and Michelle –"

"No, it's *Judy* and *Maxine*," clarified Judy as she stumbled toward the door with Mary's diaper bag. They felt clumsy as they were hastily herded to the front door.

"Alright, then. Thank you ever so much for stopping by." Aunt Row's tone had become formal and clipped and before they could respond or thank her, they found themselves on the porch with the door shut decisively in their faces.

"Let's go," urged Bev, offended. She took off for the gate. The others straggled behind her, trying to make sense of the unexpected reversal.

"Wait," Mary said, closing the gate behind her. They paused and looked back at her.

"What just happened? Don't you think that was a little odd?"

"Of course it was odd. That's why we're trying to get the heck out of Dodge," Bev said.

Mary gestured them to come back and whispered urgently, "Don't you see? She knows something. There's something very fishy going on here. I don't think we should leave just yet."

Judy glanced up at the house. "What do you suggest? Camp out and wait for Mrs. Fairview?"

"That's exactly what I suggest."

"Count me out," Maxine said. Aunt Row had made her nervous at the end.

Ann sighed and put her hands on her hips. "Oh, come on, Mary."

"Come on, what?"

"We know why you want to camp out: *Jimmy*."

"This has nothing to do with Jimmy – *James*. You didn't know he would be here any more than I did. And this is as close as we've gotten to finding any kind of answers for what has happened to us."

"You call *this* 'close'?" asked Bev sarcastically, shifting the baby carrier full of heavy books. Like Maxine, she was getting a little creeped out.

Judy agreed. "The whole thing is getting weirdsville, Mary."

"Getting?" Mary was exasperated now. "It *got* weirdsville when we woke up in the future! And we all promised to solve this mystery and no one has done *any*thing –"

To this, the girls all protested simultaneously and an argument broke out. On cue, Grace gurgled and cried. Mary jiggled the baby impatiently and it was enough to quiet her temporarily while the girls continued to stage whisper agitatedly.

Finally, Mary declared decisively, "I'm staying."

"You can't just decide for everyone," Ann rebutted with indignation.

"I'm deciding for myself. I'm going to be here when Mrs. Fairview gets back and I'm getting to the bottom of this once and for all. You're welcome to join me."

The other four girls decided for themselves, too, and left Mary standing alone with a fussy infant, diaper bag, and baby carrier.

"Unreal," she huffed to the baby. Taking the remaining books, which were her own, out of the carrier, she placed Grace in it. She gathered everything up and looked at the house. She couldn't see Aunt Row, but suspected she was cleaning in the kitchen in the back of the house. She tiptoed to the far side of the property with the driveway and made her way to the garage. "Don't start crying now," she muttered to the baby. Fortunately, the lull of the carrier seemed to rock Grace into sleep mode.

When she found the stairs up to the apartment above the garage, she was relieved to observe that the stairwell couldn't be seen from the house. She crept up the stairs and settled into the protected doorway. The small porch and railing, covered in leafy vines, obscured Mary from view from the kitchen across the garden.

"Now what?" she whispered to Grace as her nose began to hurt again.

5

Breaking and Entering

Mary dozed off and on, but woke up when Grace indicated she needed her diaper changed. As Mary struggled to remain hidden in the small space while she cleaned up her phony offspring, she was reminded of her own "necessity" and wished there was a bathroom nearby she could use. She couldn't recall Nancy Drew ever needing the ladies room in the middle of a stakeout. So much for adventure and romance.

She didn't know how long she'd been at Mrs. Fairview's doorstep, as she had forgotten to wear a watch, but the light had changed significantly and the sun was slipping like a golden egg yolk to the bottom of a pale blue bowl. Not only was Mary needing a potty break, her tummy was starting to rumble. All things she hadn't thought of when she had been so bull-headed about camping out indefinitely to wait for their teacher.

To keep her mind off of her physical discomfort, she thought about the other girls. It started benignly enough, but it took only moments before she was frustrated with each one of them. Ann, for goodness' sake, accusing Mary of wanting to stay only because of James! Well, there was no James here now, that was for sure. Bev being so ready to bolt. You know, for a tomboy, she wasn't very brave or willing to take a risk. Maxine, with whom she felt she had shared a moment and thought that maybe they were on the same page, was all too ready to bail. And Judy had completely abandoned Mary – the whole project – with hardly any provocation. On top of it all, they had left her with a baby! Some friends, indeed.

Maybe when she did meet up with Mrs. Fairview and get all the answers, she would just travel right on back to 1955 without them and let them fend for themselves. Even barely contemplated, this made her stomach do tense flip-flops. OK, she knew that wasn't a possibility. But still, it would serve them right.

Just then, she heard talking. She strained to hear where it was coming from; it was closer than the big house . . . it was coming from inside Mrs. Fairview's apartment! Mary started. Had Mrs. F been there the whole time? Mary strained to lean over the banister toward a window to see inside. There was a set of lace curtains blocking her view, but had she seen movement –?

"What are you doing?"

She teetered and almost fell over the balcony. A pair of hands grabbed her to steady her and she was sorry that the first time she felt James holding her was when she was trespassing on his aunt's property.

She gathered herself and turned to face him. "Oh, hiya," she said, smiling weakly.

"What is going on?" he asked again.

"I was actually really hoping to find a ladies room," Mary said. She couldn't believe that was the best thing she could come up with.

James glanced down toward Aunt Row's house. Lights had come on in the kitchen, but Row was not to be seen, perhaps puttering around somewhere else in her big mansion. "This is crazy, Mary. Tell me what's going on. First you show up unannounced at my aunt's house and now you're . . . *stalking* Mrs. F!"

"I am *not stalking* –" she stopped herself. What was the use? That was exactly what she was doing.

"This is the kind of thing that would really freak Aunt Row out. She lives alone, you know."

"It's not what you think," Mary said.

"You don't know what I think."

A small family of birds flitted playfully past them at eye level. How she longed to be one of them at the moment. "What do you think?"

"OK, I don't want to play games. Why don't you just tell me what you're really doing here?"

"I don't know if I can tell you the whole story," said Mary. "And I know you don't know me, but can you just trust me when I say that I really, really, *really* need to see Mrs. F? I don't know why she's in there hiding and I don't know why your Aunt Row is being vague and trying to protect her, but it just makes me need to talk to her that much more."

In a gesture of frustration, James ran his fingers through his damp, recently washed hair. "First of all, if Aunt Row says she doesn't know where Mrs. F is, then she doesn't know. And she sure as heck isn't just hanging out in here *hiding* from you. I guarantee she has better things to do. There are a lot of things going on that have nothing to do with you, you know."

Mary raised herself up with indignation, but found herself at a loss for words. James was getting the wrong idea. She stared at him in defiance, but one glance at those shimmering jewel-toned eyes of his and she melted. "I'm so sorry. I know it doesn't make any sense," she pleaded. "I just need to talk to Mrs. F, so if you can tell her I'm here, I'm certain she'll understand why."

"I'm trying to tell you. *She's not here.* I came to feed her bird."

So that was the sound from inside that Mary was hearing.

"Ohhh," Mary said. "Well, do you think she'd mind terribly if I just powdered my nose while you fed the bird?"

James's resolve crumbled and he found himself smiling at Mary's quirkiness. Who used terms like 'powder my nose,' anyway? "OK, but don't touch anything, you dig? You're not here."

Mary nodded and her ponytail bounced in agreement.

James retrieved a key from his jeans pocket and Mary picked up the baby carrier to set just inside the door.

Once inside, she looked around, surprised. It was not at all what she had expected. The furnishings were plain, simple, and beige, and there were no personal effects whatsoever. No diaries or papers lying around to shuffle through, no pictures on the walls, no shelves to hold any mementos. The only sense of life came from the orange-colored sunset glowing through the lace curtains and the large gray bird with dramatic red tail feathers squawking in the kitchen.

"Reggie watch!" screeched the bird.

"Yeah, yeah, Reggie watch," said James as he headed for the cage.

Mary followed James into the section of the apartment that was the kitchen. There were no walls dividing the living spaces between the kitchen, living room, and dining area, but the kitchen space was designated by checkered linoleum flooring and a small counter with a fridge, sink, and two-burner stove.

"What kind of a bird is that?" Mary asked.

"I thought you had to 'powder your nose'," James said, reaching under the tiny sink for a bucket of bird food. When he glanced at Mary, she looked hurt, so he said, "He's an African Grey Parrot. His name is Ike."

"I like Ike," Ike said.

Mary smiled, feeling a connection with the 1955 Mrs. Fairview. "He was a good president."

James gave her a funny look and seemed to take in her saddle shoes, full skirt with crinoline, and cotton blouse with Peter Pan collar for the first time. Mary rushed to say, "The bathroom is . . . ?"

"Door on the left." James pointed to two doors on the side wall of the apartment. The one on the left was closed, but the other was open to reveal a bedroom decorated as blandly as the rest of the place, with a double bed and simple yellow bedspread.

Mary went to the restroom, closing the door behind her. One towel hung neatly on a towel rack and a bar of white soap sat on the porcelain sink. There was nothing in the waste bin, no note detailing all the clues Mary had hoped to find.

As she washed her hands, she stared at herself in the mirror. Actually getting into Mrs. F's apartment had not been nearly as satisfying as she had hoped. In fact, worse than discovering many clues to sort through, Mary had found positively none.

Unless, Mary thought, *you count the fact that there are no clues as a clue.*

She rinsed off her face, grateful there were no traces of her earlier nosebleed, and patted herself dry. Then, before she turned to go, for kicks, she opened the medicine cabinet above the sink.

It was empty except for one thing. She gasped. It was a tube of Max Factor Strawberry Meringue, the exact same pearly pink lipstick that Mary had from 1955. Before she could second-guess herself, she swiped it and stuffed it in her skirt pocket. As soon as she closed the cabinet quietly, she returned to join James.

When Ike saw her approaching, he said, "Reggie watch."

"Does he do tricks or something? What are we supposed to watch?" Mary asked.

James shrugged. "Who knows? He's a cranky old bird."

"Cranky old bird," Ike repeated.

"Great," James muttered. "Mrs. F will be so pleased to come home to *that.*" He dumped the refuse from a tray underneath Ike's perch into a paper bag. "Are you ready to go, Mary?" James asked.

"Ready to go, Mary?" Ike echoed.

"Oh, no!" Mary said.

"Ready to go, Mary?" Ike seemed pleased to get a reaction out of Mary.

"Stop that, Ike!" James commanded. James and Mary looked at each other in a panic.

"Reggie watch!" Mary said loudly.

"Ready to go, Mary?" Ike said for a third time.

"Don't say another word," James told Mary through clenched teeth. She nodded and crept on tiptoe (for some reason) to the front door where Grace lay cooing in her carrier.

Mary knew she couldn't stay to wait for Mrs. F, as much as she longed to be there the moment she arrived. But now she believed Aunt Row's statement that it could be a day, a week, or more before Mrs. F returned.

She hauled all her various baggage to the bottom of the stairs to wait for James. Just a moment later, he joined her.

"James . . ." she started, but didn't know how to finish. She was tempted to tell him everything, but it felt wrong. It was all so overwhelming and she didn't want to drive him away for good. At least she hadn't cried like a baby in front of him for once.

Speaking of crying like a baby, Grace had been too quiet for too long and decided to exercise her lungs. That settled it for Mary; there was nothing more to say to James. She had to leave before she disturbed Aunt Row.

"Thank you," Mary said as she turned to go.

James asked, "For what?"

She heaved the diaper bag up onto her shoulder. "Just thank you."

"I'd drive you home, but I told Aunt Row . . . ."

"It's OK. Maybe I'll see you tomorrow."

When Mary walked through the front door, exhausted, the baby still crying, her mother descended on her as if she'd been waiting by the door.

"Where have you been? You don't call, or text, or anything? We've been worried sick!"

Mary looked at her, startled. Her mother was frazzled and her eyes had the panic of a wild animal. Mary hadn't seen her mother come apart at the seams like this.

"I was with . . . the girls," Mary fibbed.

"Well, you weren't with Judy because I called over to her house."

Mary was troubled by her mother's reaction. She, like all the neighborhood kids, had spent plenty of afternoons and evenings walking the neighborhood (at least in the fifties). Her mom, Nana, none of the parents had ever worried. The rule was to head home when you heard the dinner bell or a holler for your name.

"I was just around," Mary said. "How much trouble could I get in? I'm carrying a baby everywhere I go."

"I'm not worried about what *you'll* do. It's just not safe to wander around the streets. That does it, I'm getting you a cell phone tomorrow."

As Mary lay in bed that night, trying to settle her thoughts enough to fall asleep, she thought with dismay about the gadget her mother would be getting her. The last thing she needed was another mechanical anything. The only mechanical thing she needed in her life was her Singer Featherweight sewing machine, which sat right next to her bed. Her arm dropped down so her fingers could caress the smooth top of the case. It was on that machine that she had made the gorgeous blue spring dress that James had noticed and on which he had complimented her, quoting poetry.

"Remember when life used to be so simple?" she asked it.

In response, Grace, in the carrier next to the Singer, whimpered before launching into a full-on crying jag.

6

Trends, Fads and Silly Theories

"Gee, Katie, I like your skirt," Judy said. She had spent half the class trying to figure out how to introduce the topic. It was Wednesday morning, first period, computer science (which in 1955 had been a shorthand class that Judy thought would be helpful if she ever needed a part-time job until she made it big in the movies). Katie, who was a girl that was carrying around a baby just like Mary – though Katie's baby was noticeably quieter – was wearing a black skirt with a pink poodle on it. Judy had a similar skirt, although today she wore her jade pedal pushers and a coordinating flower blouse. She was actually attempting to look less '50s and was planning a shopping spree to buy modern clothes.

For a full thirty minutes, Judy tried to decide if Katie's skirt was a coincidence or an insult.

"Thanks," Katie gushed in a friendly tone. "OMG, I'm totally not dissing you, you know that, right?"

"What?"

"It's just that you guys, you know, the *Fifties Chix*, dress *so cute*." Katie scrutinized Judy's ponytails and then touched her own hair thoughtfully in a way that told Judy not to be surprised when Katie came to school the next day in pigtails and ribbons.

"We do?" Judy asked.

"Uh, *yeah*. Plus, Beverly playing for the guys' team? That's way chill!"

"Thanks," Judy responded, choosing to take it all as a compliment. For the rest of the day, she eyeballed girls, even seniors, sporting poodle skirts, pedal pushers, pencil skirts, ponytails, and saddle shoes. She decided to maybe put off the shopping spree and don her favorite poodle skirt and sweater set tomorrow instead.

Ann sat in her first class of the day, history, barely able to keep her eyes open. She had been up all night fuming about the afternoon with Mary and the girls. When they had gone to Aunt Row's house and seen James there, it was like everything went to pieces. Their mission had already been sidetracked and she should have known she couldn't trust Mary to focus with "Jimmy" in the picture. And when they were being unceremoniously ushered out of Aunt Row's home, Ann hadn't been able to help but notice that as Mary reminded Aunt Row of their names, Ann's name was glaringly absent.

As much as she appreciated moments to herself to think and paint, she did not appreciate being invisible.

"Hey, sorry to bug. I was just wondering where you got your hat?" whispered one of Ann's classmates, Carla, from her desk across the aisle.

Ann's hand went to the gondolier hat on her head. "Oh, I don't remember, sorry," she mumbled. The department store where her parents had gotten it "months" ago was out of business now.

"That's cool," Carla said knowingly and winked.

Ann would have thought Carla was ridiculing her, except that Carla wore a pencil skirt and kitten heels that looked not unlike what Ann had worn to the dance Saturday night. If Ann were at all interested in talking to her so-called friends, this would be the kind of thing she might like to mention to them.

Maxine walked from her second period math class to third period art, where she would see Ann and James. She knew that Ann had gone home in a funk yesterday and wondered what, if anything, she could do to help. She wasn't feeling so stellar herself. Being in this strange limbo was starting to take its toll. Last night when she had picked up her great-grandmother's quill to write some of her thoughts down, everything was such a jumble, she couldn't focus. She ended up just holding the quill, staring at it and whispering a one-word prayer: "Please."

A few kids who'd never spoken to her in the past called out, "Hey, Maxine," and "Hi!" She puzzled over this as she approached her art horse bench, sliding her books underneath it and pulling her art board into the niches on the bench and setting up an easel. Ann came in just a moment behind her and chose the bench next to Maxine, which made Maxine feel relieved. It was open seating; at least Ann didn't make some big statement by sitting across the room. They greeted each other, and while Ann was polite, she was perceptibly distant.

James rushed in as the bell rang. He seemed unusually frazzled and had to take the last bench, several over from Ann. As Mrs. Leach, the art teacher, started class, Maxine kept catching James's eye. He couldn't stop staring in her and Ann's direction with an anxious expression. Unfortunately, it was a quiet sketch day and not ideal for conversation, or Maxine would have asked him what was on his mind. Halfway through class, Ann couldn't help but notice James's anxious glances, too. She looked questioningly at Maxine, who shrugged. Maybe Mary had seen him last night after all and spilled the beans about why they were so desperate to find Mrs. Fairview!

Maxine was chagrined and felt her temper flare. They had never officially agreed to keep their time-travel situation a secret, it just went without saying. Or should have! As she sketched the still life in front of her, she composed a stern letter to Mary. She'd had a hard time finding words last night, but not now. Too bad she didn't have her trusty quill to jot down her thoughts. She felt betrayed by Mary's selfishness. She would have to write the letter later, even though she had hoped to give it to Mary in fifth period current events. But Maxine's next class was P.E., and then she had lunch. No matter. She felt impassioned enough; she was certain the words would still flow even if she had to write it in her French class. *Mais oui.*

"Do I have to wear a helmet in the outfield today, G?"

Beverly felt her ponytail tugged from behind and swung around to face Conrad Marshall and three of his friends. He was grinning at her.

She tried to decipher what he meant while still keeping her cool. His friends chuckled and then she realized he must be referencing her terrible play in one of the baseball games over the weekend where she had bonked heads with him in the outfield, even though he had called for the ball several times. She had been trying to impress him. She kept learning that the more she tried to impress him, the worse she looked.

"No, Marshall. And don't bother with a mitt, either, because I'll be knocking 'em all out of the park." She didn't know where it came from, but it was a perfect retort. Conrad looked fake-shocked, but pleased, and his friends hooted, slapped him playfully, and gave her approving looks.

Not a bad way to start her day. Considering the previous night had been miserable.

She wondered how she could stand to wait for practice after school.

Mary and Grace went outside and sat under a tree for lunch, Mary lost in her thoughts. She was anxious about her next class, fifth period, where she would have to face the girls that had abandoned her so eagerly yesterday. She was also worried that she had blown it with James. And as a reminder of her criminal behavior, she had the lipstick she'd stolen from Mrs. Fairview's apartment. She still didn't know why she had taken it; wasn't it enough that she'd seen it and knew about it? She'd even gone to a drugstore on the way home (making her that much later) to see if Max Factor still made the same kind of lipstick (they didn't).

As she licked the grape jelly from the corner of her mouth, Mary wished she could be getting to know James under different circumstances, when everything was neat and tidy in her life. As she considered this, she spotted the subject of her reverie making his way across the quad . . . right towards her. She held very still, feeling ridiculously like a rabbit trying to conceal itself in the wide open broad daylight. She also wasn't sure why her first instinct was to hide from him, but she knew better by the end of their conversation.

"Mary, when were you born?" He didn't greet her or ease into conversation.

Mary's mind raced. She tried to do some quick math for what the right answer should be. She could feel that she was taking too long, so she answered, "January thirteenth."

He looked at her strangely, but didn't ask the follow-up question she dreaded: *What year?*

He gently nudged the baby carrier with his shoe as he leaned up against the tree she sat under. "I think I read too many graphic novels, play too many video games, and surf the web too much . . . ."

Mary didn't know about any of the things James had just listed that he did "too much" of, so she remained silent, holding her breath, and waited for him to continue.

"I have a theory about what is going on here."

Was he going to admit that he knew she liked him? That she and Ann were fighting over him? She swallowed hard. James hesitated. After a few moments, he said, "It's too whack to say out loud."

"1995," Mary said. "January 13, 1995. I hope you're happy. A lady shouldn't have to discuss her age."

James just laughed. It was a sweet and friendly chuckle, but Mary couldn't help but infer a slight overtone of derision. "I don't know if that helped your case. Adding the year, like, two minutes late."

As a distraction, Mary pulled a swaddled Grace from her carrier, who instantly started crying. "She hates me. The computerized baby hates me," muttered Mary.

James laughed again. He bent over. "Here, let me." He took the infant from Mary and gently but emphatically rocked her from side to side. She instantly quieted. "This is a computer, so it's all based on science. The baby can't decide anything on its own. You just follow the rules and it does what it's supposed to do. It's not about getting attached to this thing that isn't real. It's just an assignment."

Once again Mary was speechless. That was a lot to chew on, considering, well . . . everything.

She reached up and retrieved Grace, placing her back in her carrier.

James squatted down next to Mary, helping her adjust Grace's blankets.

"My theory is that you time-traveled," James said quietly without warning.

Mary didn't gasp, her eyes didn't bug out, and she didn't cough loudly like it was the craziest thing she'd ever heard. She just stared at him. Through him, actually.

"Here's the part where you argue with me," James said.

"OK, you're wrong."

"Holy cow, I'm right! The outfits, the lingo, obsessing over Mrs. Fairview who's been teaching at this school since the 1950s, that whole other-worldly kind of thing you got going on . . . it all makes sense!" He retreated into his own thoughts.

Before the weight of the revelation of James's discovery settled on Mary, she had a question. "What do you mean, 'other-worldly'?"

James reddened. It was a nice change for him to be blushing. "Never mind that. This is amazing . . . do you see what's happening here?"

"Funny you should ask," Mary said. "Actually, I don't."

"I have so many questions."

"I don't feel like we should be talking about this. Whatever you think you know . . . it's not true. There's no such thing as time travel." Mary hoped she sounded convincing. She wanted to add, *But I'd love for you to explain to me how it might be possible . . . .*

"I'm not going to tell anyone, Mary," he assured her. Although in the back of his mind, he was already writing a story about it. He could *call* it fiction and no one would know the difference.

"I have to get ready for my next class," Mary said. She stuffed the leftovers of her sandwich into her lunch sack and retrieved Grace. Standing up in a hurry, she was about to rush away when she stopped, and turning to James, she said haughtily, "I don't like being teased, James O'Grady."

She didn't know where it came from, but maybe it would distract him from the time travel thing. The *very true* time travel thing that wasn't just a theory at all.

She caught a glimpse of his face as she flounced away: he was smiling.

7

False to Me in May

Bev warmed up for practice, Bob stretching next to her, in the field between the gym locker rooms and the baseball diamond.

Bev said, "Heya, Bob, what does 'G' mean?"

"Gimme a context."

"Someone referred to me as G," Bev said vaguely.

"Well, it depends on who," Bob said with a smirk.

She sighed. Why did her brothers always have to make simple things so difficult for her for their own amusement?

Just then, Conrad walked by, stretching his arms with a bat behind his neck. "Whattup, G?" he said to Bev.

Before he was barely out of earshot, Bob broke out into a big smile. "In this case, my dear Jenkins, 'G' is a term of endearment."

Before her brother could see her blush, Beverly dropped down and did ten boy push-ups.

In the bleachers, Ann and Judy were recalling fifth period in excruciating detail as it related to Mary. Sure, Mary had been in her own world lately, but Judy thought Mary should have at least acknowledged the rest of the girls. She had not even looked their direction when she sat at her desk, putting that everlasting blasted baby next to her. Mary's face had been flushed and now Judy was trying to decide with Ann if Mary had been angry or embarrassed.

"My vote is for embarrassed," said Maxine, arriving on the scene.

Judy and Ann greeted Maxine and asked what she meant.

"Well, James O'Grady was acting very odd in art class, don't you think Ann? *I think she told him our secret*; and now she's having second thoughts about it. It probably really rattled his cage and she wishes she could take it back," Maxine said with authority. She was sure about it.

"Mary would *never*!" gasped Judy. "Tell, I mean." She even took her attention off of Bob for this conversation.

Maxine shrugged and Ann shook her head. There were so many things Ann wanted to say, but didn't know where to begin, or what should even be spoken out loud. A decision was made for her when Bev's and Bob's brother, Gary, approached the girls on the bleachers, interrupting them.

"Mind if I join you?" he asked.

Before the girls could confer, Judy's typical effervescent self resurfaced and she bubbled, "Not at all!"

He smiled and sat next to Ann. Definitely a Jenkins kid, Gary had the same long face and slightly sad eyes, the same light brown, messy hair as his three brothers and baby sister, the same hazel eyes. But the similarities stopped there. The rest of his siblings were athletically inclined, while Gary, a junior and barely a year older than Bob, was focused on music and things he deemed culturally interesting.

The girls clammed up in his presence.

"So what'd you think of the dance?" Gary asked.

It took a beat for Ann to realize he was talking to her, not just raising a general question for the group. "Oh, it was swell," Ann said, adjusting her hat to shade her eyes from the blazing sun. There had been a school dance on Saturday night and Gary had asked Ann to dance with him toward the end of the evening. She'd had a hard time enjoying it, as she had been focused on where James was in the room and if he would notice she was swaying slowly with another boy. She'd prayed he wouldn't get the wrong idea! It wasn't until just yesterday, actually, that it had dawned on Ann that she should have *made sure* James saw her dancing with someone else.

Maxine stifled a heavy sigh. All this boy talk and flirting was a distraction from *real* issues. They needed to figure some things out! Well, it wasn't going to happen now that Gary had shown up to go bananas over Ann. She watched Ann and realized that Ann didn't have a clue that Gary was gaga for her. Then Maxine couldn't help but let out the long, protracted, frustrated sigh that she'd been holding in. Maybe she would just have to make peace with boys, crushes, and broken hearts as part of their "Fifties Chix" venture. She glanced out at Beverly doing warmups and thought, *Well, at least Bev has her priorities straight and isn't off her rocker over some fella.*

Dear Diary,   19th of May
   On a shelf in my room, Miss Boggs's lipstick sits next to mine.
I can't stop staring at it, feeling like it is a huge clue. But I
don't know how. I think I am fixated on it so that I don't have
to think about everything else. Like the fact that my father
announced today that he is getting remarried. I am supposed
to meet his fiancee this weekend. There, I wrote it: his fiancee.
Remarried. I wished that while we were out at the restaurant
with him, Grace would have started screaming so I could
excuse myself, but no. She was a perfect angel and silent as a
sleeping kitten. Go figure. Mother and Nana weren't even mad
about Dad getting married. In fact, Mom thought she'd make
me feel better by giving me this tiny little box, not connected
to anything, that is supposed to be a phone. How is that
supposed to cheer me up? It gives me a pit in my stomach. I
feel so trapped in this foreign land/place/time. And so alone
because the girls aren't talking to me.
   Having James tell me he thinks I'm a time traveler has not
made me feel any more settled. Now I must avoid him. I'm
sure this will make Ann happy. But if the shoe were on the
other foot, I would be heartbroken for her.
   Always,
      Mary
P.S. I'm going to make a little dress for Grace. I know she is just a
machine, like James reminded me, but I swear if she knew I don't
think she's all that bad, she wouldn't cry so much.
P.P.S. I would never write this in my diary for the baby
assignment, but I am really starting to like her. Now I know
I'm going crazy!

Dear Mary,

I know what you did and I think you should admit it to all of us instead of avoiding us. Not only do we need to hear it from you, but you need to feel the weight of the burden of telling our secret to James, of not keeping our confidence. You don't know this, but I used to watch you in social studies class and I admired you for raising your hand and almost always knowing the answers. You are brave in ways that I am not.

I know this predicament has been hard on all of us, but I had hoped that you of all of us would rise to the occasion. Dr. Martin Luther King, Jr. said, "An individual has not started living until he can rise above the narrow confines of his individualistic concerns to the broader concerns of all humanity." Until the five of us can learn to put each other first, we will never get out of this mess.

Maxine

Dear Diary,   May 19

Kip is still our sub! That's the good news. The bad news
is that means Mrs. F. isn't back yet! Maybe she'll never
come back! Maybe this is my life now. More good
news...there are still movies and there is still Bob Jenkins. Bad news: There's not a drive-in movie theater left
in town. Also, Mary is not speaking to us (or we are not
speaking to her) and toward the end of Bob's and Bev's
baseball practice today, Diane Dunkelman came to watch
and cheer for Bob. I sure wish she'd DDT.

Judy

Three more days until districts, and after we win those,
we go to the regional quarterfinals. I know I must play
one game at a time. For so many reasons. But when a
certain someone says something, or looks at me in a particular way... I can't help it—I get way ahead of myself
and I can't concentrate on the play at hand.

    -Bev

Dearest Irina,   19 May

My newest painting is going to be a bouquet of
lilacs. I think of how no matter when or where we
are, the same flowers bloom in the spring. You
probably have lilacs blooming in Belgrade, just as
we have a lilac bush in our yard exploding into tiny
fragrant blossoms. I like to imagine Bubbe, the
grandmother we have in common, smelling lilacs as a
young lady in Russia, and maybe even painting them
with the same brush I use.

There is another reason I am painting lilacs. And
it is this poem by Sara Teasdale called May that
we read in English class. It captures my feelings at
this time so perfectly, for as the springtime bursts
forth, I feel chilled by winter—the winter of friends
who betray...

"The wind is tossing the lilacs,
The new leaves laugh in on the sun,
And the petals fall on the orchard wall,
But for me the spring is done.
Beneath the apple blossoms
I go a wintry way,
For love that smiled in April
Is false to me in May."

       —Ann

8

She Said, She Said

Usually a night owl, James had to adjust his mind and body to being awake at five a.m. Being awake at five a.m. because he'd never gone to sleep in the first place was much easier than being jarred awake by an alarm, even if it was his favorite indie band programmed to rock his pre-dawn world. But his nerves had kept him up most of the night before, so this time the alarm was most welcome; at least now he could get on with his day. And it was going to be a big one.

He'd swing by the all-night copy center and pick up the 100 copies of *The Invisible Truth*, his underground newspaper; make a beeline to school to place them around surreptiously; and head back home for breakfast so he'd arrive at school at the same time as everyone else. Fortunately, the janitor, Twigler (James couldn't tell if that was the man's first name or last), was a kindred spirit and always helped James distribute the papers, stationing them in girls' and boys' bathrooms, under benches in the hallway near the office, and other strategic locations where the students would find them before the teachers or administration would. James didn't think that Twigler was particularly fond of teens, but maybe he just liked the idea of them rebelling this way – through writing and self-expression – against the school administration. Often, James surmised that Twigler was an old hippie who probably had some interesting tales to tell. Before he graduated next year, James promised himself, he'd interview old Twig and include his story in the paper.

At the end of last year, James had been "passed down" the dubious honor of editing the paper, now in its fifteenth year. Sometimes the paper caused an uproar and a witch hunt of sorts would ensue trying to determine one or any of the anonymous authors and editor; more often the paper would cause a mild stir and by the time it had been passed around in a couple of weeks, it was forgotten. This issue, James was certain, would not be the latter, thanks in large part to Maxine Marshall, pen name "Miss Thurgood" (which he thought was a little obvious, since she was associating herself with Thurgood Marshall, the first African American Chief Justice, with whom she shared a last name. But, maybe most people wouldn't make the connection. He had made a note to ask her if she was related to him).

But that wasn't what had kept him up all night. He couldn't go to sleep while he replayed over and over a conversation he was never meant to hear.

After dinner last night, he'd dropped off *The Invisible Truth* at the copy center and figured he'd check in on Ike's bird food situation, then pop in to see if Aunt Row needed anything.

He'd pulled his beat-up blue Toyota into the driveway and taken the stairs to Mrs. F's carriage house apartment two at a time. It was ironic that he'd been thinking about his conversation with Mary and her discomfort at his accusation that she had time-traveled. He smirked to himself. He hadn't known if he was for real in saying that to her or not, but her reaction had pleased him. She had tried to remain so calm, but he could see that he'd ruffled her feathers. He'd stopped short at the top of the stairs when he heard voices, then realized it was probably old Ike babbling away to Aunt Row who had come to feed him.

But before he had reached the door, he knew the other voice was not Ike's; it was Mrs. F's. And it was a tone he recognized after listening to his parents fight for years over everything from who should take out the trash to politics. He knew that Aunt Row and Mrs. Fairview were arguing.

". . . had no right, Row, no right whatsoever!"

"This is how it always goes. You tell me it's none of my never mind, then you get yourself in a bind and suddenly it's Rowena to the rescue. Do you want me to remind you –"

"Hush, I don't need you to rattle off a detailed list of every time you've saved poor little Marion. Honestly, I didn't know it was such an inconvenience for you to be a friend to me!"

Through what sounded like clenched teeth, Aunt Row had said, "Oh, stop. You know that's not what I'm saying. Now just listen, for a split second, just listen to me when I tell you, those girls were at their wits' end. They don't understand what's happening to them."

"Welcome to the human experience," Mrs. F had muttered.

"Quit that. I know you're not that cold-hearted. Ever since you and Reggie . . . ."

"Don't talk to me about him, Row. Not after you've kept that secret for all these years. And keep your voice down!"

"You won't let me talk about *any*thing! You have two choices: we can talk about those five girls or we can talk about Reggie. Up to you."

Their voices had lowered, as if they had gone into the tiny kitchen and faced the other way and a muffled conversation ensued that James had been sorry he couldn't hear. He'd managed to make out a few words: "school of life," "no going back," "gold watch," and one word that really stood out, "*Mary.*"

The word "Mary" had been particularly distinguishable because Ike had followed it with "Ready to go, Mary?" The ladies had gotten very quiet at that. He hadn't waited to hear their reactions, but had scrambled quickly down the stairs and made an intentional racket below. Then he'd called out loudly, "Aunt Row?"

She'd stuck her head out the door upstairs, keeping it otherwise closed. "Up here, Jimmy. Just checking on Ike."

"I'll come up," James had said, trying to sound casual.

"Oh, I'm fine, I'll be down in a minute. Go get yourself a cookie in the kitchen and I'll join you shortly."

And then her head had disappeared to the other side of the door, which snapped closed.

James had felt an odd sensation. His heart was beating erratically and his skin was covered in goose bumps, even in the warm and balmy spring air. He had chided himself, *What was the big deal?*

But moments later in the kitchen, he'd known what the big deal was: when he had asked Aunt Row if Mrs. F had returned, Aunt Row had gotten nervous, clattered her tea cup, and said, "No, not yet."

Now James could confirm that they were hiding something.

Mary stood at her locker, conscious once more of her life being lived without her. Events seemed to happen at her, whether she chose to participate or not. She wished she could tell the girls about her dad's news. She knew they would be righteously indignant on her behalf; sometimes when you can share something awful with someone who cares about you, it suddenly doesn't seem so awful. But after having left her standing in front of Aunt Row's house the day before yesterday, none of the girls had yet spoken to her.

Mary glanced down at a fussy Grace in her carrier and saw Maxine walking toward her. Mary's heartbeat skipped a hopeful rhythm and her cheeks flushed with joy and relief. One friend, that was all she needed. And leave it to free-thinking Maxine to buck the trends . . . .

"Hi!" Mary greeted, a little too enthusiastically.

Maxine did not respond the way Mary had anticipated. Instead, she responded with a curt, "I wanted to give this to you yesterday," and stopped an arm's length away to stiffly hold out a folded piece of paper.

"Gee . . . thanks," Mary said, not at all sure she should be thankful as she accepted the note.

"Have a good . . . day," Maxine stammered. She turned back to the direction she'd come as the bell rang for first period. Mary watched the back of Maxine's dark curled head retreat and told herself she would wait to read the note at lunch. But as Maxine rounded a corner at the end of the hall, even though Mary knew it would make her late for math, she unfolded the paper.

Mary's eyes stung as she finished reading Maxine's letter; familiar tears found their way down their usual paths on her cheeks. A combination of confusion, frustration, and sadness twisted in her belly. How did Maxine know that James thought they had time traveled, and why would Maxine think that Mary would have told him? How could Maxine accuse Mary of having concern only for herself when they were the ones that had left her standing alone (no, not alone! With a baby! A phony baby, to be sure, but still a baby!)?

Mary thought of the game girls often played at birthday parties, called "telephone." They would all sit in a circle and the first girl would whisper a sentence to the second girl, who would whisper it to the next and so on, until the last girl would say the phrase out loud. Usually, the message had gotten so garbled along the way, the girls would all roar with laughter at the final silly message. But the game had always bothered Mary, making her feel anxious. As she read Maxine's note through once more, she knew why.

Unlike her normal tidy self, Mary shoved the note in her locker and retrieved her math book. The bell rang to start class as she heaved up the baby carrier to haul around with her for yet another day.

In algebra, Ann was lost in her own thoughts when a girl behind her whispered, "I'm done with *The Invisible Truth*, do you want it?" and nudged Ann's shoulder.

Ann turned slightly to see a booklet with a light blue paper cover. The title in bold had a smaller line of text under it:

THE INVISIBLE TRUTH
Know Truth... Be Free
vol 15 issue 3

Ann panicked; what was this, some contemporary cult? She quickly grabbed the book so as not to cause a scene, and slipped it between her folder and her algebra textbook. She would dispose of it later.

But with each minute that dragged by, she could feel the thin volume calling out to her and curiosity got the best of her. As students were called up to the head of the class to work on the futuristic white board, Ann eased the book out and opened toward the beginning. Her eye fell on a poem by someone called "jackson o." She couldn't help but think of the artist Jackson Pollack, which naturally led to thoughts of James O'Grady; she'd found out recently that they both admired the abstract painter.

She Said, She Said

sunset-colored hair,
and temper's flare

    boating hat without a sail,
    deeper currents leave no trail

...passion?
    ...or security?
        love's forever question.

Ann reread it twice, but she didn't understand it. She turned the page and read more. Another poem, this one a funny limerick about the principal. She stifled a giggle and continued reading. A long editorial about unhealthy food in the cafeteria, accompanied by a clever cartoon called "Fat Kid." An angry rant of an essay, evidently directed at the writer's "evil" parents. Another nonsensical poem, this one about destiny and steam (Ann wondered bemusedly if it was supposed to be a piece on chemistry and the writer had meant to write the word "density" instead). Before she could start reading a long, hand-written article called "Useless Generation," the bell rang.

Gathering up the booklet with her other things, she thanked the girl who'd passed it to her and made her way to art class. When settling in at her easel, the book slid out from between her books. Maxine, who was approaching, stifled a gasp.

"Ohh," she said. "Where did you get that?"

Ann looked down at the book and up at Maxine. "A gal in algebra gave it to me," Ann said, curious about Maxine's reaction to the book. "I don't even know what it is," she admitted.

"It's an underground paper," Maxine said. Then, "Have you read it?"

"Some," Ann said.

Just then James O'Grady filed into the room and saw Maxine and Ann discussing the rag. He purposefully turned his attention from them and sat farther away than usual.

As the bell rang, Maxine asked quickly if she could borrow it. Ann agreed. "As long as I can see it again. There's a poem in there that's too deep for me, but I want to figure it out."

9

Still Waters Run Deep

Meshuga was sprawled out in the shade, but she was still panting.

"Spoiled little thing." Ann shook her head at the little white family dog. Ann, too, had found a shady place in the garden, and set up her easel with a fresh canvas, relishing starting her lilac painting. The oil paints on her palette were simultaneously forming a film and sweating. She had to work quickly, but it was better this way. She'd read that van Gogh used to deliberately make himself uncomfortable, layering on wool sweaters on a hot day (much like today) so that he would be forced out of himself and into his art.

Ann pondered this idea of "being forced out of oneself." She had been forced out of herself when coerced to work with the other four girls on the Travel to Tomorrow assignment; she'd been forced out of herself when she'd woken up fifty-five years into the future; she was being forced out of herself every time she crossed swords with Mary about the boy they both liked.

Her family had been forced out of their homeland, selfhood, and identity. She only hoped that she wouldn't be forced out of herself so much that she would share in van Gogh's tragic fate: failed artist dead at thirty-seven of suicide. How could an ending so grim come to an artist whose paintings were so colorful and full of life and vitality? Ann shuddered, even in the hot sunshine.

Maybe if van Gogh had hung on long enough, he could have seen some of his dreams come to fruition and his artwork sell. Of course, he could never have imagined that some day, on the list of highest priced paintings ever sold, he would have seven, totaling $670 million! Maybe Ann needed to take a cue from Vincent and try to hang on long enough to see some good come from her struggles. Either that, or abandon his philosophy altogether and get out of the heat!

For the second time in the recent past, she thought of Anne Frank's diary again. She'd nearly memorized it. Though the diary had begun to make her too sad to consider anymore, her heart still sang the same strain that Anne Frank's heart did: *"I want to be useful or bring enjoyment to all people, even those I've never met. I want to go on living even after my death! And that's why I'm so grateful to God for having given me this gift, which I can use to develop myself and to express all that's inside me!"*

She grasped her favorite paintbrush, the one her grandmother – her bubbe – had given to her mother and her mother had passed on to her. It was the only thing of her bubbe's that she had, and it felt like a lifeline to her lost grandparents and to 1955. With the brush loaded with paint, she lay in the background of her painting, the biggest shapes and colors, dividing her attention between her composition and letting herself think about James O'Grady. She was no Beverly Jenkins, but Anna

Branislav still had a competitive streak like anyone else. *Is that the source of my growing feelings toward James?* she wondered. Was she really just trying to "win" his affections over Mary? Or did she truly admire him?

Readjusting her palette and applying a large shiny swatch of brilliant spring green, Ann recalled the first time she'd seen James. It wasn't love at first sight; he wasn't exactly your typical dreamboat. But he'd . . . grown on her, like a painting developing. You might not see it all at first, but as more colors came to light, the existing colors took on new life. She smiled at her memory, though it hadn't been all that meaningful at the time.

At the beginning of the semester, she'd been nervous to be taking an art class. It was her first one, though she'd been painting on her own for years. She was worried the class would prove that she had been painting "wrong" all along, or worse, ruin the creative process for her to the point where she'd lay her bubbe's paintbrush down and forget all about it. Creating paintings connected her to her grandmother and the rest of the family she'd never met; it was her link to her heritage and she couldn't afford to sever it.

That first day of class, she had been the first to arrive and chosen an easel right up front, her own quiet act of bravery. She'd watched everyone come into the classroom. Maxine Marshall, one of about three or four black kids in their school, had glided in. Ann had smiled at her when she approached, supposing any new class for Maxine was probably a challenge. There was an appealing calmness to Maxine. Not only was she pretty and polished, she appeared confident, right when and where she could have reason to be apprehensive. Ann had noted that they were the only two girls wearing pants.

James O'Grady had arrived then, unlike the two other boys who were joking and laughing with each other, maybe overcompensating for taking an art class. James had seemed genteel, much older for his age. Certainly not because of his looks; he had a youthful freckled face and red hair slicked back properly. His flannel shirt had been tucked tidily into his jeans, which were rolled up to reveal shiny penny loafers. He had come right to the front and sat next to Ann, while the other students had filled up the back of the classroom first. He'd had a calm composure that had reminded her of her father.

Still waters run deep, she thought at the memory of a 1955 version of James. Then something tickled in the back of her mind, and a line from the poem she'd read earlier that day surfaced: "deeper currents leave no trail . . . ." Was that what the author meant? And then the line before it emerged in her mind's eye: "boating hat without a sail."

Was it possible . . . ?

Just then, Meshuga yelped and jumped up, startling Ann back to the present; Ann's little brother, Alex, and his friend, Franco, rounded the house shooting water guns at each other. Irritated at being interrupted, annoyed that they were playing with guns, and just generally miffed that Franco was Diane Dunkelman's little brother and Alex's best friend, Ann snapped at them angrily.

"We're just *playing*," Alex responded.

"With guns?" Ann huffed. "Does Mom or Dad know?"

"They don't care," Alex said, sending a stream of water Meshuga's way. She tried to catch it in her mouth.

"Yeah, all guys play with guns," Franco piped up.

"Not *all* boys," murmured Ann. She thought of the uncle they'd never known, Alexei, her Dad's baby brother and Alex's namesake, who had been shot by Nazis in Yugoslavia when he was just about Alex's age. Vexed, Ann gathered up her paints, palette, and easel to take inside. In her hurry, she smeared the painting on the front of her blouse.

"Now look what you've done!" she shouted at the naughty boys.

"Geez, take a chill pill," Franco said.

It was all she could do to not break the canvas over his head.

What had she just been thinking about "still waters"? Well, so much for *that.*

Mary stood in front of the open fridge. She was hoping for some celery sticks and peanut butter like she used to have after school, but now the kitchen was filled with unrecognizable and unappealing items. Organic skim milk, for example. Yuck. It only reminded her that their rich-tasting, thoroughly opaque and creamy milk was no longer delivered by the friendly Mr. Ocasek. When Mary was a little younger, she'd time it just right to be waiting by the milk box on the porch when the milkman arrived and he'd offer her an ice cream bar as a treat.

Today was the first time in weeks she'd been home after school, having no friends to meet with, nothing to dig into at the library, and no Mrs. Fairview to stalk. Mary found being at home in the afternoon surprisingly peaceful. Her mom was still at work at her real estate office and Nana was with the younger kids. Grace was snoozing in the dining room. Despite not being a big fan of fruit, unless she was using it to bake a pie or whip up a gelatin salad, Mary settled on an apple.

Her solitude was dashed when the door from the garage burst open and her little brother Danny flew in like he'd been sprung from a trap. "Hi!" he called as he clumsily knocked the baby carrier on his way to the living room to watch TV. Grace's cry ripped through the air.

Exasperated, Mary went to the baby as her sisters, Patty and Maggie, and Nana came through the door. Nana greeted Mary warmly, happy to see her home and among the living for once. Mary responded with a hello. She missed Nana, too, but not because they didn't see each other as much; more because Nana was a different person than Mary had known her to be in 1955.

Patty and Maggie put a couple of bags of groceries on the counter, and Nana followed suit. As Mary began to collect her belongings to head to her room, Maggie stopped her.

"Can I see the baby?"

"It's not a real baby," Mary reminded her.

"I know," Maggie said, gently pulling back the blanket to see Grace's face. Grace continued to cry an intimidating howl, but Maggie said, "Can I hold it?"

"It's a *she*," Mary said, faltering in her determination to escape. She caught a glimpse of Nana's contented expression as she watched the girls out of the corner of her eye while putting the groceries away. It had been a long time since Mary had had much of an interchange with anyone at home. She'd spent all her time and energy on her so-called friends, and look where that had gotten her. She'd been "here" – or maybe it was "now"

– for over two weeks, but she felt like everyone living in this house was a stranger to her.

She pulled out a dining room chair for Maggie. "Here, it's easier if you sit. She's as heavy as a real baby." Maggie placed herself carefully in the chair and stuck her arms straight out in anticipation. Her skinny stick legs swung out from underneath a little purple ruffled skirt she wore; on her feet were pink glittered high-tops and her T-shirt had a large white cartoon cat on it. Mary knew that, with the exception of how she was dressed, Maggie and her twin, Patty, were mirror images of Mary at their age. The unruly red hair, the smattering of freckles, the eager green eyes. Mary's heart softened a bit as she really looked at her little sister for the first time in a long while.

"Support her neck and head," Mary advised, placing Grace gingerly into her little sister's arms.

"I know. Remember, I used to hold Danny?" Maggie reminded her. For so many reasons, it seemed ages ago. But it was true; both Maggie and Patty had been wonderful big sisters to their squirmy baby brother.

As Grace settled in to Maggie's arms, she stopped crying. Maggie brightened. "Hey, she likes me!"

Mary smiled.

Maggie talked to Grace in a cloying "baby" voice that Mary couldn't help but find endearing. Maggie stopped and looked up at Mary. "Did you make this dress for her?"

Mary blushed. It was stupid to have made an outfit for her computerized dummy.

She didn't respond, but Maggie said excitedly, "Maybe she *will* make it for us, Nana!"

Nana brushed her silver hair out of her eyes as she put a bag of rice patties in the pantry. "Well, ask her, then."

"Mary, will you make us mac and cheese? You always used to make it. You know, before . . . ."

"Before what?" Mary asked, curious.

"Before you were so mad and sad all the time," Maggie responded matter-of-factly. She turned her attention to the baby, tickling it and touching its cheek.

"I'm not mad . . . or sad . . . ." Mary's defenses shot up, but fell again. Of course, what else were they supposed to think? Not only was she never home, but when she was around, she had zero tolerance for anyone in her family. It wasn't their fault that she was totally different, was it?

"Of course I'll make mac and cheese," Mary said.

In the other room, the TV blared as usual, but Patty and Danny were curled up together on the sofa. She could be thankful for that small favor, at least.

"Nana says you're sad because of Daddy," Maggie offered conversationally. Mary looked at her grandmother, who looked apologetic. Not waiting for confirmation, Maggie continued. "Remember when Danny and Mommy and Daddy all came home from the hospital? We were all a family."

Mary did remember, but she wondered how different her memories were from Maggie's. Nana had come to stay with them when Danny was born and Mary had been in heaven. They had played games, baked together, crocheted a tiny pair of yellow booties for the baby, and watched the very first episode of *I Love Lucy*. It had been like a little vacation, the highlight of which was Danny's arrival as a tiny bundle in the arms of his daddy. At that point, Mary had been sure of her dad's love for her, so she hadn't been concerned over how he doted on his first and only son. Even then, she'd had a funny feeling that there was something missing for her dad, and maybe baby Danny was just what he needed. She had hoped.

But before Danny had even spoken his first words, her father had moved out with little explanation. Mary had felt foolish because she wasn't in the adult club to talk about it; surely she couldn't understand. But she *did* understand. She knew the night he left that she wasn't only losing her father, she was losing her mother. Because he was taking the best part of her with him. Mary had never found the words to tell her mom that she knew that. In the years since, she had tried to act mature to show her mom that she understood; she had tried to prove that she was grown up enough to handle the family emergencies and that they didn't need a man around the house after all. But now, after acting so disrespectfully in the last couple of weeks to her family, especially Nana, Mary feared she had wasted any progress in being seen as mature and capable. With each day that passed, Mary was getting further and further away from whom she hoped to be . . . or be seen as.

She reassured herself out loud so Maggie could hear, "We're all still a family. It just looks different, I guess."

Maggie nodded with a grin. And then their special fleeting moment together was gone. Maggie hopped off the chair, shoving the baby at Mary and hollering at her siblings in the other room, "I don't want to watch this!" while grabbing the remote and changing channels.

Both Grace and Danny began to holler in protest.

Mary was about to allow herself to get depressed, but she saw Nana laugh and shake her head. "You said it. We're all still a family," she reminded Mary cheerfully.

After writing in her baby journal and attempting to do her math homework, Mary came downstairs to make macaroni and cheese, as promised. She looked in the kitchen closet, but could find no apron. "I'll be right back," she murmured. She returned to her room and pulled out a pink gingham ruffled apron she'd made recently with her Singer Featherweight. As she was tying the apron's long pink ribbons on her way downstairs, the door-bell rang. The kids were zombies in front of the TV and acted as though they hadn't even heard it. She sighed and opened the door.

There stood James O'Grady. Mary was too stunned to speak, other than, "How did you . . . ?"

"Googled your address," James said, and then, catching sight of her retro apron, muttered, "Look who I'm saying that to."

"I . . . how? Why . . . ?" Mary stammered.

"Hi, by the way." James offered a sheepish smile.

"Oh. Hello. Where are my manners? Would you like to come in?" And then as soon as she had asked, she regretted it. The place was a mess, the kids were, well, monsters, and he was a boy. In her house.

To make matters worse, her mother's car pulled into the driveway. She hopped out, calling, "Yoohoo! I got off work early when I heard you were making dinner. Oh, hello! You must be Mary's *friend*."

Mary cringed at the tone in which her mom said "friend." It was too full of meaning. Now James would think she was a misfit for sure.

Ms. Donovan approached the front door instead of going in the garage and introduced herself. Mid-intro, some silent alarm went off and she said, "Sorry, gotta take this," and touched a little metal chewing gum-sized contraption attached to her ear.

"Mrs. Allen!" she cooed, pushing past Mary and James at the front door. "We got an offer . . . ."

"That's my mom," Mary said lamely.

"I know this must really freak you out, having me come over like this. I didn't have your cell number and I know you're not on Facebook and I had to tell you something," James said. He was freshly showered and Mary guessed he had just come back from track practice.

Mary invited him in and suddenly the kids were awakened from their trance.

"Hi! What's your name?"

"Are you Mary's boyfriend?"

"You have red hair, too."

Mary flushed and apologized profusely for the children's behavior.

Nana came in then, briefly introduced herself, and asked if Mary and James might like some privacy. Ms. Donovan had returned from her phone call and suggested Mary's room.

In unison, Mary and Nana exclaimed, "No!"

Mary was flooded with relief to be on the same page as Nana. She and James went out to the back patio, Mary placing the apron on the dining room table by the baby as they passed by. She only hoped Nana would keep the ankle-biters from gawking out the sliding glass door at them.

"I couldn't find you at lunch," James said.

"I was in the library, reading," Mary replied.

He wanted to ask if she was reading *The Invisible Truth*, but lost his nerve. Had she seen the poem he'd written? Had she identified herself in it? James had an uncle on his dad's side who was a writer in LA for a cable TV show. His uncle said that he "wrote" real people that he knew all the time and they never recognized themselves. Problem was, James didn't know if he wanted Mary to know he'd written about her or not. Plus, the little detail that the other girl in the poem was Ann would most likely not sit well with Mary. He was relieved that at the moment, he had another item to discuss with her.

Mary sat on a chaise lounge, smoothing her skirt, and then hopped up suddenly. "I'm so sorry. I didn't offer you a refreshment!" she apologized. James, who had been looking somewhat nervous, relaxed into a smile at that.

"I'm fine. You don't have to entertain me."

His little simper rattled her cage. Annoyed, she sat back down. "Pardon me. I was just . . . ."

"I know. Thank you." He tried to calm her. It didn't take much for Mary's feisty side to show itself. "I came because of Mrs. Fairview."

"I know you think I'm 'stalking' her – your words – but if you could just trust me –"

"I didn't come over here to insult you or to accuse you of something!" James's tone was impatient.

"Fine," Mary said with cool politeness. She felt reprimanded. If James had something to say, then he should just get to the point.

"She's back."

Mary leapt up and stood facing James, closer than she meant to. "You saw Mrs. Fairview? But she wasn't at school!"

"I know, which I thought was weird because I heard her last night. I didn't actually see her, but I heard her. She was arguing with Aunt Row."

"Did they know you heard them? What were they arguing about? Where were they? What time was this?" Mary had so many questions. Finally, a clue, or some little ray of hope. . . .

"They were in Mrs. F's apartment, and I'm not sure if they knew I heard them. Afterward, Aunt Row lied right to my face, telling me that Mrs. F still wasn't back! They mentioned you . . . and then Ike said 'Ready to go, Mary'." James did his best parrot impression.

"No!" Swept up in some mix of shock and delight, Mary laughed and unconsciously put her hands on each of James's arms. They realized it at the same time. Before moving away, she stared into his eyes and he gazed back. For a split instant, there was no 1955, no 2010, no past or future, just an eternal moment *now* . . . and just the two of them in it. Mary felt as if an entire conversation had passed between them with just one look. Overwhelmed, she abruptly jumped back, pulling her hands away. She thought of Ann, as her habit had been, and then became flustered. She didn't owe Ann anything, didn't know if they were even still friends. But regardless, Mary just wasn't that type of girl. The type of girl that would disregard even a former friend's feelings.

"What did they say about me?" Mary said, forcing herself to recover.

"They mentioned you and your friends and Aunt Row said something about how it's not fair."

"What's not fair?"

"This," James said pointedly. "What you're going through. *You know.*"

"What it is again that you think I'm going through?" Mary asked. She wasn't trying to be coy. But especially after Maxine's accusing Mary of telling secrets to James . . . .

"CS Lewis wrote, 'The Future is something which everyone reaches at the rate of sixty minutes an hour, whatever he does, whoever he is,'" James quoted. He paused. "Everyone except for you, Mary. You jumped ahead to your future."

Mary had had her mind boggled for the last two weeks, and more so every day. James's knowing something, or thinking that he knew something, was surprisingly unhelpful. "Did you and Maxine Marshall have some kind of conversation about your little theory?" Mary asked.

"My 'little theory'?" James was taken aback. He faced toward the backyard with his arms across his chest. There wasn't much to look at in the Donovans' garden. It was nothing like Aunt Row's. Mary's house had a small backyard, littered with the kids' abandoned toys, and bordered by a vinyl fence on three sides and houses on each of those sides. "I'm not a total idiot, Mary," he huffed. "Between you, Aunt Row, and Mrs. F . . . I swear . . . and *no*, I didn't have a conversation with Maxine. But I've been the recipient of her curious looks and I've read . . . . ." He stopped. He wasn't ready to open up the subject of *The Invisible Truth*, even to mention Maxine's essay. Maxine hadn't come right out and said that she had come fresh from the 1950s, but there was a style to her writing, and things she spoke of about the '50s that couldn't just be gleaned from a history book. Nonetheless, he wanted to steer clear of Maxine's article in case it led to the poem he had written. He could see now the problem with writing anonymously. It emboldened you to make public statements that maybe shouldn't be public.

Confused, Mary said, "You read . . . ?" She was thinking, of course, of Maxine's scathing note to her.

Dropping his arms and turning to face her fully, his eyes twinkled. "Maybe this is wrong. OK, it's wrong . . . but something amazing is happening here and I want to be a part of this. I know it's selfish. But . . . I kind of am a part of it, for whatever reason. Ya know?"

Mary of course desperately wanted James O'Grady to be a part of "this," but she knew their shared desire probably came from different motives – he, intrigued with time travel and adventure; she, intrigued with him. The question was, should she just ignore that detail and jump in with her whole heart and hope they eventually ended up on the same page?

"The girls think I told you something that I shouldn't have told you," she blurted. "Maxine . . . she thinks I can't keep a secret."

James let out a low whistle. "Maxine, huh? Interesting coming from her."

"I feel like you're talking in code."

"I know, I know. Ignore me. Just . . . let's put it this way. How can I help?" James said earnestly.

"I need to find Mrs. Fairview."

On an already overcast day, the sky seemed to darken, and Mary got a chill. James stepped closer, hesitated a moment, and then put his arms around Mary. "We'll find her, then."

10

Future Mrs.

Rowena grabbed her best friend's left hand and stared. "He sure didn't get this at Jenkins Hardware," Row marveled.

May Boggs stared at the huge engagement ring on her finger, probably even more amazed than Row. "I love it, and I love him – but is this really me?"

Row gestured to the ornate gold watch on May's wrist. May followed her gaze, pulled her hand back and touched her diamond ring and her wristwatch alternately. "You know that's different."

Row laughed, tossing her shimmering fair hair in the moonlight. "How so?"

They sat on the patio at midnight. Row's father and stepmother were sound asleep, but there was the faint drone of the television on in the parlor behind them. Row had been waiting up for May to come home, knowing that this was the night she would be announcing her engagement. Since May had started teaching, she'd rented out the little apartment over the garage of Row's parents' house, much to May's mother's chagrin. Row knew that now that

May would be marrying Reginald Fairview, it would all change. The Fairviews owned a lot of property all over the county, and Reggie probably already had some beautiful acreage near the river in mind where he would build a mansion for his bride.

May didn't answer Row's question, choosing to think of it as rhetorical, but removed her cat-eye glasses to pull off her false eyelashes and rub her eyes, then plucked the hat off of her head. "These hairpins are killing me," she sighed, grasping them out of her curls and using her upside down hat as a holder for the pins and lashes.

Not ready for the magic and fantasy of youth to give way to the mundane details of adulthood, Row said, "Tell me again how it happened, May." It was just like the old days, a sleepover at Row's house, when all their adventures were only imagined. Row was even in her white cotton nightgown. It was a balmy spring evening, the sky punctured by starry gems, while a few adventuresome bats flitted through the garden. How many summer nights Rowena, Marion, and Emily had camped out in this garden would be impossible to count. Beautiful raven-haired Emily Jackson, who was long gone, and whom Row still missed every day. The three of them had had adventures together that no one could have imagined possible. Row and May had taken those experiences as something that bound them all together, but they had frightened Em – the bravest of the three of them, or so they had thought – away for good. Certainly, with what Em had experienced, she couldn't be faulted. Eventually Row and May had stopped talking so much about Em, stopped wondering about her and hoping for her return. It hurt too much.

Marion brightened and sat up straight, eager to recount the story of her Prince Charming's proposal. She told how Reginald had brought her a bouquet of heavily perfumed white roses and lilies and escorted her from the upstairs apartment down to his spanking new

1955 red and white convertible Buick Roadmaster. He'd opened the car door for her, helping her not to bump her flowered hat as she settled in. As he pulled the car out of the driveway, he'd apologized that he didn't have a horse and carriage to pick her up in instead.

May wanted to say something about how he had always been her knight in shining armor, but she'd never been particularly quick or confident with words, so instead, she just smiled and basked in his attention. Her white-gloved hands folded in her lap, she listened as Reggie turned up the radio, crooning "Love is a Many Splendored Thing" to her over the wind rushing into the car. She felt like a teenager again . . . except for the fact that she'd never been asked to ride in a car with a boy when she was a teenager.

The sunset provided the perfect backdrop – smears of magenta and purple and orange – to the light pink summer wool suit May wore. Her mother had chipped in to help her buy it from Stix, Baer & Fuller – or, as everyone called the popular department store, Grand Leader – downtown. Mother had been all too happy to support May's dressing like a lady to impress Reginald Fairview. As May described her evening to Row now, she realized that of course her mother had known that Reggie would propose; he had asked May's father for her hand.

May described going to the nicest Italian restaurant in her old neighborhood. She was secretly pleased that Reggie wanted to take her there, and not somewhere downtown where she would be less likely to be seen by people her family knew. Usually not one for show, or who enjoyed being in the spotlight, May felt that tonight was the exception. She wanted to focus on something sweet and special and romantic; something to take her mind off of other things.

May related everything about her evening: the table up front with yet more flowers, how Reggie got down on one knee, pulling a ring from his suit pocket, the entire restaurant coming to a standstill to hear her reply and then cheering when she said yes.

She didn't tell Row about how her thoughts had drifted to her students then, especially the five girls who were forever changed because of her, and she couldn't yet determine if it was for the better; would one of them, or even all of them, run away scared like Emily had done? She chose not to voice how she wondered at the practicality . . . or even possibility . . . of living between two worlds at once. Being Mrs. Marion Fairview would be a full-time job, a full-time identity. And she had already committed to a full-time identity that was pulling her in too many directions.

May's story continued, detailing dessert – the little pink cake Reggie had commissioned that had "Future Mrs. Fairview" scripted in white frosting on top. The word "future" had made her choke on her ice water; it was a word that made her jittery in a way that Reggie could never understand and reminded her of the secrets she was keeping from him.

As May described how delicious the cake had been with its decadent raspberry filling, she absently caressed the gold watch on her wrist. Row touched her gently, interrupting her. "It all sounds dreamy, May."

"I wish Em were here. She would like Reggie, don't you think?"

"I know she would," Row said. Row was feisty and argumentative, but she was as kind as could be when the occasion called for it. "You ready for bed, to have sweet dreams?"

May nodded.

Long after they'd said goodnight, Row had padded down the hall on the second floor to look out the guest bedroom window in back to see that the lights were still on in May's apartment.

Row doubted she was having sweet dreams because May never slept with the lights on.

11

It's Complicated

May picked up the phone and placed it gingerly back in its cradle at least twelve times. She was exhausted from her latest argument with Row, but as was often the case, Row had been right. It didn't mean that Row understood everything that was happening (she rarely did); in fact, Row was notorious for taking an overly simplistic view of everything. But maybe May made everything too complicated and should take a cue from Row. She had been threatening to do that for more than half a century.

May sighed and looked at Ike. "Ike. You make the final decision. Should I call Mary?"

Ike squawked, "Ready to go, Mary?"

May couldn't help but laugh. That brief moment of levity was all the encouragement she needed. Besides, she wanted to know how it was that Ike had learned that phrase . . . .

She grasped the phone and this time dialed without hesitation and let it ring on the other end.

Mary nestled Grace in next to her under the quilt. She knew it was ridiculous, snuggling a machine as if it were a real baby, but she had tried it last night and not only had Grace not cried, Mary had also felt a little comforted. She had needed it after the news of her dad's engagement and tonight she needed it – if only to keep the baby quiet! – to think through every detail of her afternoon with James and what it all meant.

Just as she was remembering how it felt to see him standing on her doorstep, an electronic ringing cut through her reminiscing. The sound was a familiar one; she had heard it earlier that day in the library during lunch. It had been Mary's mom calling her on the cell phone she had given her. It had been the first call Mary had gotten on it and all she had wanted was for the noise to stop. Mrs. Donovan, on the other hand, had seemed overly thrilled to be talking to Mary in the middle of the day for no good reason other than the fact that she could.

Once again, Mary wanted the sound to stop and jostled the baby in the process of retrieving the phone from her desk. Plus, she had given the number to James. Maybe, just maybe . . . .

As she answered the call, Grace let out a wail of annoyance. Mary reminded herself, *Only two more days, kid*, but oddly didn't feel consoled by that fact.

"Hello?"

"Mary?"

Mary hadn't heard that voice in nearly a week, but knew it once who it was. "Miss Boggs!"

"I'm awfully sorry to be calling you so late," Mrs. Fairview apologized ("late" being the case on more than one level).

"I don't mind. You can call any time. I've – we've – been wanting to talk to you." Mary suddenly found herself overcome with nerves. This was her big chance to get all the answers she was seeking and make it all right not only for her, but for the four other girls. She didn't know what to ask first, or how to go about it without scaring off Mrs. Fairview.

"I know. You can thank James. And his Aunt Row. They . . ." Mrs. Fairview chose her words carefully. Not coerced, but ". . . *helped* me get in touch with you. I'm not one for the telephone, however, so I was wondering if I could meet you tomorrow after school. At my apartment? I believe you know where that is."

Mary blushed in the dark. Grace continued to fuss and Mary wanted to stuff her under a pillow, but knew that smothering her school project would result in a huge markdown in her grade.

"We'll come right over after school," Mary agreed eagerly.

Mrs. Fairview cleared her throat. "Actually, Mary, I'd like to meet just with you. By yourself."

"Oh, but Miss – Mrs. Fairview, the other girls –"

"I'm afraid that it needs to be just you or there can be no meeting. I know this must be hard for you to understand, but –"

"Hard for me to understand?" Mary cried, unable to contain all the emotions bubbling up in her.

"Mary."

"You don't know what it's like!"

"I know more than you think I do. Just come tomorrow. Alone, please."

And before Mary could respond, argue, or even apologize, Mrs. F had clicked off.

In addition Grace's audible unrest, now there was a whole new gaggle of questions for Mary to lose sleep over.

"You still up?"

Bev jumped back from the mirror over her dresser, embarrassed. She had been inspecting her face and hair, trying to determine if there was anything interesting there for a boy to look at. Her bedroom door was open just a crack and Gary tapped on it. She was in her PJs, her usual sleeping uniform consisting of an old T-shirt passed down by one of her brothers.

Gary hadn't seemed to notice what she was doing, just that her light was on.

She invited him in, throwing on a robe.

He looked around her room, smiling. "Dang, guess I haven't been in here in a while. A *long* while . . . ." He scrutinized her All-American Girls Professional Baseball League pennant and an ancient Cardinals pennant.

Beverly was self-conscious about her room. Its contents and decor were the only aspects of her 1955 life that had come along with her into the future, and she hadn't exactly been entertaining guests in it. Even her mother hadn't been in to clean, having never been home to do any cleaning. Bev found herself learning how to use the newfangled clothes washer and dryer and dishwasher. Otherwise, there would be no clothes to wear or dishes to eat off of.

"So, what's going on?" Bev said, attempting to be casual and divert her brother's attention from their surroundings. Out of habit, she picked up her Louisville Slugger to fiddle with. It was her security blanket in ash form. She loved the feel of it in her hands; it was so natural to have her fingers gripping it as if it were an extension of herself, just another appendage. She craved the sound it made when it connected with a fastball. In fact, Bev was so attached to the bat that she had special permission from Coach to use it at practice and at games; everyone else used a metal bat that Bev found soulless and depressing.

"Vinyl? Awesome!" Gary said, picking up one of her records.

She grabbed it from him protectively and snapped, "Can I help you with something, or are you just trying to ruin my beauty sleep?"

Gary flopped down onto her bed and looked up at the ceiling, looking like he was settling in. He sighed. "Just checking in."

While Gary was the most communicative of her brothers, she still had the feeling he wanted something and hadn't dropped in just to chat. She balanced the bat straight up in the palm of her hand as she eyed him suspiciously.

He rolled over to face her. "Are you nervous for the game this weekend?" Then, seeing the look on her face, he laughed. She knew he hadn't come in to shoot the breeze about baseball. "OK. I wanted to ask you about your friends. *One* friend."

"Mary?" Bev asked. Mary had been on her mind a lot. They had split, leaving her on that old lady's sidewalk the day before yesterday, and the other girls had been sore at Mary ever since. Bev had tried to not be distracted by it all, trying to keep up with her studies, practice for the upcoming game, and, well, day-dream about a certain teammate.

"No, not Mary. *Ann.*"

"Ann razzes your berries?" Bev asked in surprise.

"Razzes my –? Say what? Anyway, I find her interesting . . . ."

"Hm." Bev should have known. At the dance last week, Gary had insisted on tagging along and had even asked Ann to dance. Bev hadn't thought too much about it, assuming Gary was just trying to be polite. She thought back to 1955, when Ann's mother, Mrs. B, had been their cleaning lady; had Gary had his eye on Ann even back then?

"So, I know this is very grade school of me and all, but . . . does she ever talk about me?"

Bev put the bat behind her neck, draping her hands over either end of it, causing her elbows to stick out like chicken wings. "Umm . . . we don't talk about boys that much." Well, it was almost true. *Bev* never talked about boys.

Gary continued to pepper Beverly with questions about Ann Branislav – her interests, whether she liked anyone at school, what Bev thought of the idea of Gary asking Ann out on a date. Bev did her best to remain vague. She knew that Ann was hung up on James O'Grady, but didn't think it was her place to divulge this detail to Gary. Besides, things were a little complicated with the whole James O'Grady thing, with Mary sweet on him too.

Beverly recalled the very first time she had officially met Anna Branislav, long before the Travel to Tomorrow project. They had been at the same school for ages, but never crossed paths much due to Ann's quiet demeanor and interest in art and Bev's tomboy tendencies. Ann's mother, Mrs. B, had been cooking and cleaning every day for the Jenkins family for as long as Bev could remember. Finding out that Mrs. B had a family of her own had shocked Bev, like when she had discovered that her teachers had a life outside of school when she saw her fourth

grade teacher at her dad's hardware store on a Saturday afternoon.

It was in fifth grade and Bev and her brother, Bob, then a sixth
grader, were walking home from school. Bob's friend, Dave, was
walking with them and they were debating who was the preferred baseball team, the Browns or the Cardinals. Bev was
aware of a girl from her class following behind them at a distance. When they crossed the street, she crossed the street.
When they turned a corner, she turned a corner.

Finally, when Bev and the boys arrived home, the girl went
right up the front walk behind them. Bev waited awkwardly at
the front door to see what she wanted, while the boys didn't
pause, but made a beeline to the kitchen for cookies and milk.

"Hi," Bev said to the girl, whose name she knew was Anna.

"Hi," Anna said. "I'm here to see my mom. My daddy is sick
so he can't take care of me today."

Just then Mrs. B came to the door behind Bev. "Hello darling," she greeted her daughter. Bev was a little hurt to hear Mrs.
B call another girl *darling* in that sweet maternal way. "Beverly,
you remember my girl, Anna?"

"Ann," Ann corrected, ducking her eyes shyly.

"We go to school together," Bev said. She wanted to be
friendly and make Mrs. B happy. "Come on in."

On the way to the kitchen to get snacks, Bev asked Ann if she
wanted to have a catch outside. Ann declined politely. Her
pretty features and dark glossy hair made her seem too delicate
for outdoor games. "Hopscotch?" Bev offered hopefully.

"No, thank you. I'll just do some sketching indoors while I
wait."

Bev couldn't imagine anything more boring and instead played kickball with her brothers and Dave in the backyard. By the time she came in to wash up for supper, Mrs. B and her daughter had gone home. Bev felt like she had missed an opportunity, but wasn't sure what she should have done instead. The next day at school, she made sure to say hi to Ann, but there was no connection there and so they had always remained distant though courteous.

And now their lives were intertwined in ways Bev never could have imagined, little of it having to do with Mrs. B, who no longer worked *for* Bev's mother, but *with* her in a business they co-owned.

After getting no satisfying answers from Bev, Gary said, "OK, I get it. You don't wanna run interference for your friend. Don't tell her I was asking about her, all right?"

"Deal," Bev said, relieved.

"So, how's it going with Conrad Marshall?" Gary asked conversationally.

"*What?*"

"Ah, c'mon, baby sister. Everyone knows you're crushing on him."

"Everyone?" Bev was alarmed. "Who is everyone?"

"Bob told me. If he knows, it's gotta be pretty obvious to everyone else."

"Well, I am not 'crushing on' Conrad Marshall. He's an arrogant actor, a real drag, and a phony! I don't like him at all! What's to like, anyhow?"

Gary laughed heartily on his way out of her room. "Keep it up, Bev, I totally believe you."

Exasperated, she slammed the door behind him.

Judy finished rolling her hair and dashed into the living room. A bowl of popcorn and a stick of chocolate chip cookie dough (it came in a stick! She could just eat it raw!) were waiting next to the remote control, along with her autograph book. The little white leather book that held her father's last written words to her was her link to the past that she couldn't let go of. She wanted it next to her, even when she wasn't in her bedroom, which was decorated in 1950s nostalgia. It reminded her that what was happening was real and not made up. It helped her remember who she was and who she dreamed of being.

Judy shooed the cats off the sofa and plopped down. Now that she knew how to turn on the TV and the satellite – which had hundreds of channels 24 hours a day – she was in seventh heaven. She watched old TV shows on reruns late into the night. Last night, after watching a hilarious *I Love Lucy* episode (from 1957!), wherein Lucy moves to the country and gets overrun by baby chicks, Judy watched in a near-trance a marathon of a show called *Happy Days* that was old to everyone else but new to her. And it was all about the 1950s, so she loved it. The opening song was one of her favorites, "Rock Around the Clock," and reminded her of when things were good with her friends, last Saturday at the school dance and at the slumber party at her house so long ago when they had danced to the song over and over until they'd dropped.

While Judy watched TV, she had the laptop computer open and searched around a virtual world called the Internet. It was mind-boggling and definitely overwhelming. She had the Internet to thank for finding out about how her dad had been killed in the war since her mom hadn't wanted to talk about it. Tonight as she went down the rabbit hole of the Internet, her mind spun and her eyes burned, but she couldn't seem to stop. She was amazed that she could go into a little white window in her computer and type almost any question she could conceive of, and pages and pages of answers would come up for her to peruse! Her mom came out and asked if she was going to bed anytime soon, but Judy was still up even hours after that.

She even found that "face book" everyone was talking about and she thought she might stake a little claim on it.

Step by step, as Richie and The Fonz stirred up trouble in the background, Judy set up her own account on the website. When she put her school name in, the computer started asking if she knew people at the school! And then . . . there it was. Bob Jenkins. She clicked on his name and was asked, "Add as Friend"? Of course that sounded great. Moments later, a little window popped up with a picture of Bob and the words, "You're up late!"

Judy jumped and the bowl of popcorn flipped over, sending a blizzard of corn through the air. Her cats, Desi and Dragnet, already annoyed at having been disturbed when she'd taken over the sofa, gave her dirty looks from across the room.

"I think it's him! What should I do?" she asked them in a loud whisper. In response, Dragnet went back to sleep and Desi yawned disinterestedly.

"Hey," she typed back. Nothing. Then she tried pressing "Enter" and her "Hey" made a little sound as it flew through the air, across the neighborhood, instantly to Bob Jenkins.

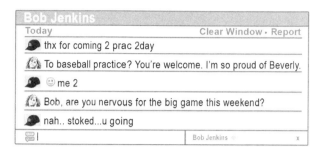

Judy could hardly believe it! Her palms were sweaty and she was shaking. She was nervous for several reasons, not the least of which was the fact that she could barely understand Bob's terrible typing. "u going"? Did he mean "Are you going to the game?" Judy wondered. She played it safe:

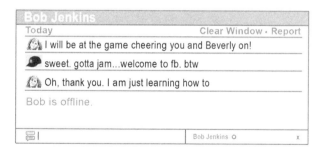

She let out a squeal and grabbed a pillow to cover her mouth, then danced around the room, crushing some of the popcorn into the carpet. She didn't care! That was one more conversation with Bob Jenkins! Even if it wasn't in person or over the phone.

She tried to calm herself enough to work the computer keyboard. She clicked on Bob's picture and a page of information came up, including:

Relationship Status:

It's Complicated

Other people had "In a Relationship With . . ." and a name listed, but not Bob. There was no Diane Dunkelman listed under his relationship status. This time Judy hopped up on the sofa to do a jig as the cookie dough got jostled to the floor with a thud; she didn't even try to conceal her squeals of delight.

From the other room, she heard her mom call out, "Jujube, pleeeease . . . some of us have to work in the morning. . . ."

"Sorry, Mom!" she called back.

But she wasn't sorry. Things were looking up. Girls at school were starting to dress like her and Bob Jenkins all but wanted her to come to his big game.

Nope, she wasn't sorry at all.

12

Cruel to be Kind

The minutes and hours dragged by. Every time Mary looked up at the clock, she swore it had actually moved back in time. *Well, that would be novel,* Mary thought sarcastically, considering she had been forced fifty-five years forward in time overnight.

She had given up focusing on her schoolwork. Everything going on in the rest of her life crowded out studies and academics! Not only was she obsessing over her meeting with Mrs. Fairview and the fact that she had to go alone, she replayed James's embrace and wondered what it meant and if she should feel guilty for Ann's sake.

By the time she got to fifth period, she had nearly forgotten the girls weren't talking to her, so when Judy said "Hi," Mary responded with a casual greeting back before realizing she was being spoken to; she gave Judy a questioning look.

Judy looked sheepish and passed Mary a note.

Mary,
Did you really tell James our secret? That doesn't sound
like something you would do, even if it was James
O'Grady. Can you get together after school? We can go
to my pad.
Judy

Mary heaved a sigh of relief that Judy hadn't joined in with the others in accusing Mary of spilling the beans to James. But as soon as she had felt a little solace, she felt guilty. She wrote back,

Judy,
Thank you for writing that. I miss you girls. You're right, I would never tell
our secret. But I think he knows something is up. I wish I could see you
after school today. Can the five of us get together tonight? I have something to tell all of you . . . If the others will agree to see me. I don't know
yet, but I hope it is good news.
Your friend,
Mary
PS Grace says "hi" and that she misses you!

Mary hoped her note was cryptic enough, but not too con-fusing. She had added the "PS" to make Judy smile, which it did. She had also scribbled out where Judy had written James's name, just in case the note were to fall into any one else's hands.

There was no opportunity to talk to Judy or any of the other girls that period because Kip kept them all busy as he lectured about societal customs. Even when he asked a question, he didn't wait for an answer, but barreled on through having a one-sided conversation with himself. Mary thought this might be the longest class period of her life and wished Grace would wake up and scream so Mary could excuse herself. But, uncooperative as ever, Grace snoozed away peacefully.

Judy felt much better, like things were getting back on track. She didn't think Mary would have let the cat out of the bag, but it was hard telling. She might as well ask, though. She missed being with all the girls and felt like there was no one to tell that Bob had "spoken" to her through the Internet.

After school, as she gathered her things at her locker, feeling confident and cute in her pink and black poodle skirt that the popular girls were eyeballing, Judy felt someone sidle up next to her. She jumped when she realized it was Diane Dunkelman.

"Oh, hiya," Judy said nervously. She couldn't help but notice that Diane was the only one of the popular girls not wearing any 1950s-styled clothing or accessories.

"Hi. Judy, right?" Diane's voice was syrupy sweet, making Judy instantly wary.

Judy looked around for a friend to save her or for an excuse to run away.

Diane laughed a soothing chuckle. Didn't snakes charm their prey before pouncing? Judy's heart skipped a beat.

"Look, I totally know I haven't been, like, the sweetest to you or anything, but I just want you to know that I actually really like you. I mean, my boyfriend Bob says you're like a little sister to him, so I should probably be nice to you if it makes him happy . . . ."

Judy tried to control her facial expression. Swallowing Diane's words was like biting into a piece of rotten fruit. *Boyfriend? Little sister?* "He said that?" Judy coughed.

"Oh, yeah, he thinks you're neat. Maybe we can hang out some time." Diane smiled at her sympathetically. And then she leaned in conspiratorially. "Since we're going to be such good friends, can I let you in on a li'l sumpin' on the hush-hush?" Without waiting for an answer, she continued as she brushed her long blonde hair behind her ear and whispered, "I shouldn't be telling you this at all – oh, the girls are gonna kill me – but look. The fifties thing you got going on? Everyone's kinda . . . making fun of you." Diane gave Judy the saddest face she could muster and Judy's cheeks burned a bruised pink.

Judy quickly looked away before Diane could see her eyes glisten with tears.

"I mean, I think it's cute and funny and all – your adorable little outfits – but I think getting everyone to laugh at you behind your back is totally uncalled for, you know?"

"Well, I appreciate you telling me . . . all of that. Girls can be so unkind. But it doesn't matter. I was in on the joke all along. Thanks anyway." Judy finished retrieving the books she'd need for homework and slammed the locker to hurry off.

She got around the corner before the tears started to fall and she heard Diane call out, "Bob and I really hope you can make it to the game!"

Judy walked home crying, not sure which books she'd grabbed and which she was missing. It didn't matter. She'd be spending most of her time this weekend shopping for new clothes anyway. And a big block of her time had just opened up since she *absolutely* would *not* be going to Bob's baseball game.

Mary did something she'd never done before: she left her books and her homework assignments in her locker. On purpose! It was the last weekend she had the baby and there was too much on her mind anyway. The only thing that Mary was taking home – besides Grace and all her necessary baby paraphernalia – was the blue booklet she'd seen kids reading the last couple of days. It looked to be some kind of underground paper, which could be a hoot to look at. Not that she'd have time to read it, or even cared, considering she was on her way, at long last, to meet with Mrs. Fairview.

She'd gotten a block away from school on the long walk toward Aunt Row's property when a blue car pulled up next to her. Cars nowadays made her nervous and this one seemed to come right to where she was on purpose, so she flinched just a bit. But then she glanced over and saw James at the wheel, waving wildly.

"I bet I know right where you're headed. Need a lift?"

She faltered, knowing she needed to meet with Mrs. F alone, but realizing, too, that it was thanks to James she had gotten the meeting at all. She felt like she was part of some big top-secret caper, and wondered for the millionth time why things needed to be so complicated. Finally, her desire to get a ride with James in his car trumped everything else.

"Sure, thanks." She shrugged.

Once he'd helped Mary and her baby things into the car, James ran back around to the driver's side and pulled his seat belt on. He glanced at the blue booklet in Mary's lap.

"What's that?" he asked innocently.

Mary said, "I haven't the foggiest. All the kids are reading it, so I thought I should. Haven't you read it?" She was surprised James would be asking her about it; he always seemed to be in the know.

"I guess I've heard about it. How much of it have you read?" He didn't take his eyes off the road. There were a lot of students milling about the neighborhood streets; it seemed like on Fridays, the student population multiplied and the nice weather kept them lingering.

"None of it, yet. You say you don't know what it is?" Mary asked.

James changed the subject quickly. "Are you nervous to see Mrs. F? Are you meeting the other girls there? What are you going to ask her first?"

Mary's thought instantly shifted to her social studies teacher and her friends. "I'm very nervous. She told me to come alone." Mary wrung her hands on top of the book in her lap. She didn't answer his last question because she didn't know herself.

"That's weird, don't you think?" James said.

Mary nodded in agreement. "Everything's weirdsville; I shouldn't be surprised."

James broke into a wide grin and nodded slightly at Mary's use of the word *weirdsville,* as if he'd made a mental note.

When they pulled into Aunt Row's driveway, James said with a mixture of excitement and trepidation, "Let's go."

Mary paused. "I think she wants me to come *alone.*"

"Oh. OK, but tell me everything. I still have a lot of questions, you know. You haven't told me *anything*."

Tell that to Maxine, Mary thought.

She got Grace out of the backseat along with the diaper bag and carrier. When she tucked *The Invisible Truth* under her arm, James said, "You don't need to take that, do you?"

The funny look Mary shot him made him drop the subject.

"Should I wait, or do you want to call me?" James asked.

"I don't know how to call you."

James asked for her cell phone and gave her quick directions on how to look at the received calls and dial him from there. It was very simple, but she looked bewildered. He laughed and said maybe he'd just go check on Aunt Row and Mary could find him when she was done.

He was being so attentive; Mary knew it was because he was interested in the riddle that had become her life. With every waking moment she spent with him, she liked him more and wished that he could like her the same way, and not just because she was a time-traveling novelty.

As they parted, she had a sinking feeling that their quick, informal "See ya soon" should have been much more of a goodbye. If Mrs. F sent Mary back to 1955, there was no telling what Mary's and James's friendship would go back to being like. Her stomach turned into itself and became a hard clump; she felt as though she'd swallowed a bowling ball. At the top of Mrs. F's outside stairwell, she turned to see James for what she was scared was one last time, but he was gone.

She knocked on Mrs. Fairview's front door and Grace woke up and howled at the top of her lungs.

Mary held her breath as the door opened.

Ann was lost in her own thoughts walking home from school after picking up her little brother. Alex chattered beside her about some fantasy science fiction game, but Ann didn't hear him. She wouldn't have understood much of what he had been talking about even if she did pay attention. Still, it was comforting to have him speaking to her instead of listening to his earphones and cutting her out as he had been doing.

"I told him he'd have to do better than that to get to the seventh level!" Alex said.

"Mmhm," Ann agreed absently. Then she noticed a familiar site crossing the street up ahead. "Hey, isn't that –? Judy!" she called out.

It was Judy; she turned slightly, waving, and then hurried forward.

"Well, what in the world?" Ann muttered and called her again. "*Judy!*" She murmured for Alex to keep up and she took off at a jog to catch up to her friend.

As they approached, Alex looked Judy up and down in her pink and black poodle skirt, pink blouse, and saddle shoes and shook his head.

"Judy . . . what . . . ?" Ann wondered why Judy had been trying to avoid her.

Tears were streaming down Judy's face, but still she attempted a bubbly, "Oh, hiya!"

Ann put her arm around Judy. "What's happened?"

Judy had promised herself she would just avoid her friends so that she wouldn't have to tell them the truth: that they were the laughingstock of the school. She wasn't going to tell Ann in that moment even, but she was terrible at keeping secrets. "You know how everyone is dressing like us at school?"

"Why's that?" Alex said with a look of mild disdain. Not to be mean. Just because he was a little brother.

"Cut the gas!" Ann ordered. "Yes?" she said to Judy.

"It's all a joke. They're making fun of us!"

Ann had thought it was peculiar, too, that girls were asking her where she had gotten some of her clothes and accessories and were starting to wear pieces that could have come from her own closet. But she found it hard to believe that it was all just to mock her and the other girls, the Fifties Chix.

"What makes you think that?"

"I have it on good authority, from the horse's mouth –" she couldn't help but allow herself a little pleasure at thought of Diane Dunkelman having the mouth of a horse "– Diane Dunkelman said the popular girls are poking fun at us. And Bob thinks of me as a *little sister!*" With the last two words, Judy began to sob. "Life is so cruel!" she choked out dramatically.

"There, there," Ann said, holding her friend. She understood exactly how Judy was feeling.

Ann had been planning on lighting candles tonight for *shabbat*, deeply missing the family's Jewish tradition and hoping it would bring her some comfort. But now she knew she needed to put aside her own plans and feelings and be there for her friend. For all of her friends, truth be told. Her family hadn't been observing the Sabbath and they certainly wouldn't miss it tonight. She hoped God would be forgiving about it.

"I think we need to make fudge tonight at your house. *All* of us," Ann suggested gently, thinking of all the kosher laws she'd be breaking.

Judy brightened up and blew her nose in the handkerchief Ann had offered. "That would be swell, Ann."

Now Ann just had to get up the guts to face Mary.

"I know you don't understand any of this, Mary," Mrs. Fairview began, at a louder volume than normal. Her student's "baby" was howling. She couldn't use it as an excuse to get out of this conversation. She pressed on, unsure of how much she should say. The whole truth, she now knew all too well thanks to Row, would be daunting. But not enough truth – she knew that part thanks to Reggie – would be cruel.

Ike piped up, "Ready to go, Mary?" and Mary's face flushed.

Mrs. F ignored Ike and continued, though she suspected there was a story behind Ike's new vocabulary. She started out with what she thought were encouraging words, a way to break the ice with warm sentiments. But Mary's expression indicated her utter lack of interest in what was sounding even to Mrs. F herself like a collection of flimsy platitudes. Mary wanted answers; of course she did. Mrs. F knew it because she'd been there herself. When Mrs. F paused only slightly, Mary burst in with an emotional, one-word demand:

"Why?"

Mrs. F said, "Do you remember what I told you girls in the soda shop? What I made you promise?"

"To be friends . . . in fifty-five years," Mary gulped.

"And where are your friends now?"

"You said I had to come alone –"

Mrs. F didn't want to provide Mary a one-way ticket on a guilt trip, but she had to make Mary understand . . . had to make sure she did not make the same mistakes young Marion Boggs had. Mary flushed and looked down as she admitted that she and her friends had not been getting along so well.

"Why do you think that is?"

"A boy," Mary had said quietly, a subtle question mark at the end begging for dissent.

Mrs. Fairview's heart went out to her student. She could see that Mary didn't yet comprehend the reason this all had happened, didn't see the bigger picture and her place in it. She understood what Mary was going through more than Mary could possibly know. She knew what it felt like to want two things – to live two different lives – with equal longing. She wanted to be able to tell Mary what she should do; she wanted to make it all better, easier. But that would be like trying to help a caterpillar out of its cocoon. It only ensures the butterfly won't be strong enough and will quickly die away. There were great things ahead for Mary; but there would be challenges, too, and there was only so much Mrs. Marion Fairview could do. And for the second time in as many weeks, the thought crept in that maybe she had made a cosmic mistake choosing Mary – and the other four.

But like the other time Mrs. Fairview had pushed down that doubt, she reminded herself that she didn't have the answers herself, as her disarrayed-at-the-moment life clearly evidenced.

So how could she expect Mary – or Ann, Judy, Maxine, or Beverly – to know any better?

"If he's distracting you and putting a wedge between you and your friends, you need to consider if he's worth it," Mrs. F said frankly. She hated her words as she saw the pain they caused Mary.

Mary's mouth dropped open. "What?"

"You have to ask yourself if he is part of the plan."

Mary put aside the no-more-James implication for a moment when she heard the word "plan." "The plan? What's the plan?" Mary asked excitedly.

"The plan, darling, is to stay friends with the girls as you promised. Think about what you need to do to make that happen. I know you can do it." She looked at the panicked look in Mary's eyes. If only she could better help Mary see all the puzzle pieces and how they fit!

Mrs. F sighed, "There are bigger things at stake than puppy love." As soon as she said it, she'd regretted it. What kind of a teacher or mentor was she to belittle what she knew Mary was feeling? Why couldn't she take some of this burden off of the girls? But again, she thought of the beautiful butterfly who could fend for itself, having started its new life fighting to be free.

The only problem with that analogy was that it hadn't worked for Emily Jackson. All the more reason it needed to work this time. Now.

Mary's face had burned anew, but not with embarrassment; this time it was with indignation. Mrs. F found this spark encouraging.

"I hardly know anything more than you do about all this, Mary, I assure you. But what I do know is that you need to make some hard choices." Mrs. F knew that Mary wasn't the only one facing some hard choices. She herself was in the same boat. Did love and truth have to be mutually exclusive? Must she choose one over the other?

"But, Mrs. Fairview . . . " Mary's voice caught. "Why? Why me, why us?"

With genuine affection, Mrs. F brushed a loose strand of Mary's red hair behind her ear. Hair that was only a shade more strawberry than Mrs. F's – Marion's – had been at that same age. "Time will tell, sweetie. Time will tell."

Mrs. F couldn't help herself; she watched, hidden behind the curtains of the front window, as Mary and the baby left. As she suspected would happen, James came bounding over with his youthful, optimistic lope. His gestures and features reminded her of a boy she used to know and adore: Wally Nolan, Row's big brother. Her heart constricted with a stab of pain. She wondered if Row saw the resemblance and was reminded of her tragic loss every time she looked at her nephew.

A brief conversation between James and Mary ensued, and though Mrs. F could not make out the words, she could have written the script. Mary's body language told the story, as did James's shrug of frustration as she walked away without him.

"You'll thank me," whispered Mrs. F. "I *hope* you'll thank me," she amended for the sake of precious honesty.

13

Away from the Future

When Mary was nearly home, her cell phone rang several times. Worried that it was James, she didn't answer it, but after it kept ringing, she finally shifted Grace in her arms and took the call with trepidation. She'd have to find something to tell James, she just wasn't ready yet.

But it was Judy calling. Her nose sounded stuffed up. Judy had called Mary's house and Nana had been surprised that Judy didn't already have Mary's cell phone number and had given it to her.

Mary barely heard a word Judy was saying, she was still so dumbfounded by her encounter with Mrs. Fairview. But Mary knew her friends couldn't be avoided any more than she could avoid telling James she couldn't see him anymore, so when Judy reminded Mary of the invitation to come over, she accepted.

She finally found a good use for the cell phone when she was able to call Nana to tell her she was going over to her friend's house.

Mary could have taken the baby's ominous screaming at Mrs. Fairview's as some sort of sign. On the walk over to Judy's, Grace went to sleep and gave Mary some quiet time with her own thoughts: exactly what she didn't want. The only thing this baby was good for was bad timing.

Marion Fairview could not bear another sleepless night; she was a zombie during the day and she knew that the school administration was expecting her back for the last few weeks of school. She knew too, though it was meant to be a surprise, that they had been planning to throw a big happy retirement party, complete with a school assembly in her honor featuring a "This is Your Life"-inspired presentation. They would probably invite Reggie and maybe even Row. The thought of such public recognition was enough to keep her up at night, but that wasn't all that was on her mind.

Most nights she was able to fall asleep because she was so exhausted, but her dreams were so vivid that she awoke in a frenzied state and whatever rest she may have managed was dashed. Therefore, she did whatever she could to stay awake to avoid dreaming.

But that day she'd spoken to Mary and watched the poor girl's heart break right in front of her, and she couldn't bear her conscious thoughts and slipped into a fretful slumber. Her dreams that night weren't imaginary hallucinations, but detailed memories.

The wedding was on the last Sunday afternoon in June. There had been barely enough time to throw it together; if May had had her way, she and Reggie would have eloped and spent the week at a cottage in the Ozarks. But Reggie's mother and May's mother wouldn't stand for a quiet wedding, much less a secret one. Mrs. Boggs's tenacity and Mrs. Fairview's money made for a nonnegotiable situation for the bride: she would have an extravagant gala of a wedding that would be the talk of the town whether she wanted one or not. May's guest list had gone from thirty to four hundred in the space of one conversation between the two mothers.

For every pre-wedding event, Row had been at May's side. Row, who laughed loudly and could make witty small talk, who put herself in the spotlight so May could try to blend into the background. Row, her maid of honor, who acted like life was a big tickle, despite the hand she herself had been dealt. Sometimes May wondered if Row should have ended up with Reggie. They had a lot more in common, and truth be told there had been a moment where they could have been an item. But for reasons about which May was unclear, Reginald Fairview had chosen her to be his bride.

May stood in front of the full-length mirror in the church's bridal chambers and stared at herself. She carefully applied the lipstick she had worn the night Reggie proposed, Strawberry Meringue, instead of the deep scarlet shade her mother had bought for her. Beyond her favorite lipstick, she could hardly recognize or feel like herself buried in the heavy ivory satin, ornately pearled and beaded wedding dress with a ten foot train. For one thing, it was a sweltering day and the dress felt like it weighed a thousand pounds; for another thing, her long veil and perfectly done-up hair looked unnatural with her goofy four eyes. Her mother had begged her not to wear her glasses, but May couldn't see a foot in front of her without them and she sure wasn't going to marry Reginald Fairview without being able to look into his eyes. May hadn't had a choice about much else: the cake, the venue, the date, the dress. She could at least choose to see Reggie the moment he became her husband!

Her bouquet sat on a table by the door. The floral detailing on the front of her dress was almost a waste because her large nosegay of creamy white roses and lilies was so oversized, you couldn't see the front of the dress when she held the flowers. She would have been happy with a white leather Bible and a single rose, but that idea, like all of her others, had been pooh-poohed.

As she whispered what was to be her new name while staring at herself to see if it fit, Row popped in the door.

"Oh, you look absolutely divine!" Row raved. But of course, it was Row who looked divine in her coral tea-length off-the-shoulder party dress. Her suntanned skin and glowing blond hair had been a source of May's envy for years, and were no less on that day. Row had pointed the dress out when she, May, and the two mothers had been shopping for May's wedding dress. May's previously adamantly practical mother had gushed to Row, "It's lovely! Of course, dear, whatever you want," words she hadn't uttered even once to her own daughter about the wedding.

"I wish we could trade dresses," May said wistfully.

"Then you wouldn't be the bride, silly. This is your day," Row said, straightening May's intricately detailed train.

May finally broke down and admitted to her friend, "It just feels all wrong. I don't know if it's because Em's not here, or because it's nothing like I imagined . . . . "

Row pulled a handkerchief from her little satin purse and offered it to May. "Now don't cry, you'll steam up your peepers."

As usual, Row made May giggle.

"I want a marriage, not a wedding," sighed May, getting to the heart of the matter.

"Then a marriage ye shall have, Maid Marion," proclaimed Row. "Only first, you have to make your mother happy by having this bash. Then you can be married to Reginald Fairview as much as you want . . . and as long as ye both shall live!"

Once again, Row had made May giggle. She was so grateful her best friend was there; she didn't know how she would have made it through what should have been the happiest time of her life. It felt more like Row was giving May away than her father was.

Outside the door, the organ music swelled from the church. May's heart skipped several beats and then rocked inside her chest double time to catch up. She grabbed Row's arm with her sweaty white-gloved fingers. There was sheer panic in her eyes. "What if this messes everything up? What if it isn't part of the plan?"

Row got serious in a hurry and grabbed May right back, holding her wrists in a surprisingly tight grip. "Listen to me, you've got to stop that. You love Reggie and he loves you. That is the plan. No more nonsense about the plan –"

The door opened then and May's father came in. He was bursting with pride in his white tuxedo jacket and black pants and tie. He told May how he'd just been having a smoke with his soon-to-be son-in-law. "He's as cool as a cucumber, sweetheart. He can't wait to marry you," were his words as he took his daughter's arm.

"Thanks, Daddy," May said, holding back tears, referring to him as she had when she was so much younger. Row gave her a wink and went to retrieve the bride's train.

At the door of the church, May's mother waited to be escorted down the aisle by one of Reggie's cousins. When she caught a glimpse of her daughter, she beamed a rare display of unimpeded joy. May knew the smile was borne on a wave of relief more than anything: May could be checked off her mother's list of worries.

"Just perfect," May's mother whispered and couldn't help but make her way over for one last embrace before her only daughter headed down the aisle. As she pulled away, she reached up and snatched May's glasses.

"Mother!" May hissed.

"You'll be fine," her mother assured her, dissolving into nothing more than a hazy glob.

Then, from what May could tell, the church doors opened and the processional started. Only a moment later, her father moved her forward and she passed through the heavy oak doors. She was desperate to look up the aisle to Reggie, but she could only vaguely make out forms around her. This was all wrong.

She stopped.

The bridal march blared all around her, so loud it made even the heavy fabric on her dress quiver . . . or maybe that was her nerves. Her father tried to pull her forward, but she resisted.

Suddenly, she heard a "No!" yelp above the music and as she wrenched herself from her father's grasp, she realized it was her own voice. In a moment of unthinking panic as he tried to stop her, her dad planted his foot heavily on her train. There was a horrific tearing sound as the train separated from her dress.

May lunged for the door, toward the light, and stumbled down the church's front steps. She made her way out to Reggie's red Roadmaster, which was waiting for the newlyweds with a driver inside. She dove in the backseat and ordered the driver to go. Alarmed, the chauffeur hit the gas and the car lurched forward, away from May's future.

In one inexplicable moment of optical clarity – or maybe it was her imagination – she made out Reggie on the front steps of the church with his arms toward her, calling her back.

When Judy welcomed Mary with open arms and sobbing, Mary wondered if Judy could read her mind. Judy apologized for falling apart and helped Mary inside with the baby. Mary noticed that Judy's living room wasn't as tidy as usual; there were dishes and various wrappers and containers littered on every surface and three blankets twisted and tangled up together on the sofa, whose pillows were strewn on the floor. The blinds were drawn and it didn't smell particularly fresh. Mary felt the strong urge to open a window, but didn't want to offend Judy – who was obviously feeling a little raw – right off the bat. Mary was relieved that she was the first to arrive, feeling that it gave her some sort of home field advantage.

But first things first. Mary asked after Judy, who declined to elaborate other than saying she was glad that her girlfriends would all be getting together again. Mary began straightening up the place without asking permission and Judy didn't seem to mind. They chit-chatted while Mary cleaned and Judy played with Grace. Both had much to say, but held back, waiting for the others.

Mary's nerves tingled, wondering who would show up first, Maxine or Ann. Both were frosted at her for what she had determined were imaginary reasons. Still, the thought of facing them was no less intimidating. Like ripping off a band-aid, Maxine and

Ann arrived together. They were noticeably friendlier toward Judy than they were toward Mary. Maybe if Mary had had a tear-stained face, she could have garnered a little empathy, she thought to herself bitterly (and then chided herself for feeling mean). But Mary, amazingly, hadn't shed a single tear since she left Mrs. Fairview's apartment. She was too shell-shocked.

Mary excused herself to go feed and change the baby, hoping to take long enough for Bev to arrive after her baseball practice. Mary closed herself into Judy's room and, after caring for the baby, remained in Judy's shrine to 1950s Hollywood. Mary noticed that under nearly all Judy's favorite stars – James Dean, Marilyn Monroe, Natalie Wood, a young Elvis Presley – Judy had added a handwritten note: "RIP." This tugged at Mary's heartstrings and she felt something loosen in her: she wanted to break down and weep as Judy had done, and as she herself had been doing regularly; but she also felt the need to stay strong for her friends.

At last she heard Beverly arrive and Mary felt safe to join the group. In the living area, blinds and drapes were pulled back and windows were mercifully open. Mary got a warmer reception from Bev, who always seemed the most unmoved by conflict.

Judy, still sniffling, announced that she had a surprise and led the girls into the kitchen. On the table were five soda glasses with long spoons, and on the floor around them pink and black balloons.

With a quivering lip, Judy said she wanted them to feel like they were back in the soda shop the day they had promised to be friends forever. Mary's jaw dropped open. Had Mrs. Fairview gotten ahold of Judy, too?

"Cool," Maxine said, inspecting one of the glasses.

"Boss," Bev agreed, picking up a pink balloon and batting it playfully.

"It's lovely," Ann told Judy, giving her a hug.

Mary just stared at Judy, wondering.

"Don't you like it Mary? You look sore," Judy said.

"No . . . it's perfect . . . more than perfect. I'm just surprised is all."

"Well, it was supposed to be a surprise. Who wants root beer floats?"

Judy and Mary scooped vanilla ice cream and poured root beer, then distributed the floats. They sat at the table in silence, slurping and thinking until Mary couldn't take the loaded silence any longer.

"I didn't tell James our secret, but he somehow figured it out. And I saw Miss Boggs."

"Where did you see her?" gasped Judy, while Maxine said, "How did James figure it out?"

"What did she say?" Ann wondered out loud, avoiding the subject of James, and simultaneously Bev asked, "Did you talk to her?"

"She was avoiding us, I think, but James found her . . . or Aunt Row did, but they convinced her to talk to me," Mary began before being cut off by more questions.

"Why was she avoiding us? And why didn't we get to talk to her?" Judy squealed, and the others asked questions in a similar vein.

"She called me and told me to come alone," Mary said patiently. She couldn't blame them. She would have been near-frantic if one of the girls had seen their teacher without her. "I went to her apartment . . . and she reminded me that we promised to be friends forever." Now the tears Mary had been holding in began to leak out as she recalled the other portion of their conversation about James – that she should stop seeing him because she was a bad friend when there was a boy in the picture. She cried a little harder at the prospect of having failed her friends when she had to admit, "I didn't find out anything."

"Did you ask her about our Travel to Tomorrow project?"

"Or if she was the one who did this to us?"

"Did she say anything about why she's aged but no one else has?"

"Or our 1955 bedrooms?"

They pounded her with questions, as eager as ever for answers.

Mary hung her head, shaking it slowly no. "I couldn't remember anything to ask her and besides, she wouldn't let me talk; she kicked me out real quick."

"It's OK, you did the best you could." It was Ann who put her arm around Mary. Ann – who liked James O'Grady as much as Mary. Ann – who didn't yet know that Mary had had a friend in James for the space of a heartbeat and that now it was over.

"What do we do now?" Maxine asked.

"This is it," Bev theorized. "We're stuck here and we might as well get used to it."

"That's why we're going shopping," Judy resolved. "We can't keep dressing like this . . . and expect people to take us seriously."

Ann sat back down, still holding Mary's hand. Mary had settled into a melancholy, her tears drying up, but her heart still hurting. Ann recalled Judy's earlier revelation that their clothing was the butt of a joke. "I agree with Judy," she said.

Maxine, Bev, and Mary looked at the other two, surprised. Before they could protest, Judy told them, "I was told that we are the laughingstock of the school."

"Who said that?" Bev demanded.

Judy ducked her head and admitted, "Diane Dunkelman."

"Diane Dunkel –? That chick can drop dead twice for all I care!" Bev stormed. "She's nothing but jealous, Judy!"

"She has nothing to be jealous of," Judy said. And then she choked out, "Bob thinks of me as a *little sister*."

Bev couldn't speak for her big brother, but she knew Diane Dunkelman well enough. "You can't believe anything she says."

"Still, I'm going shopping. Who's going with me?"

The girls were oddly quiet, all thinking the same thing. What if they did this, were they accepting their new lives? Was there no going back to 1955? Did they even want to?

One by one, they all agreed. "I'm in." And to reseal their deal to stick together, Mary encouraged them to hold hands and they once again promised, "Friends forever."

Then Judy and Mary both bawled, waking up Grace, who joined them.

14

Stolen

Mary was not typically a big fan of shopping for clothes, since she preferred to make them, but she was grateful that Saturday morning to have a distraction from thinking about James. Well, from thinking *exclusively* about James, anyway. He had called her the night before, undoubtedly to check on her meeting with Mrs. Fairview, but of course Mary hadn't answered it. If she had heard his voice, she could have so easily disregarded her vow to stop seeing him; and what if there were some rule that she would be breaking by letting him get any closer? What if Mrs. Fairview had been telling Mary in so many words that if she focused 100% on her friends, it would help them get back to 1955?

When she had asked her mom and Nana if she could go to the department store, they were so thrilled, they had both given her money.

"Two hundred dollars!" she marveled over and over again. She had even tried to leave the computerized baby with Nana, but Grace got fussy whenever Mary's electronic bracelet got too far out of range. So Grace was coming along, too.

It was a clear, hot day, perfect for Bev's baseball game later on. Mary didn't know if she should go since James would most likely be there; though of course she wanted to cheer for Bev. Even though the weather was nice, Nana drove Mary to Judy's house, where they would go together to meet the others.

Mary wasn't talkative, but that didn't keep Nana from chatting non-stop. She told Mary that she really liked James and thought he was a fine young man. She mentioned that even Mary's younger siblings had taken to him when he had come over the other day. She said she was sorry that James couldn't have stayed for dinner to taste Mary's scrumptious macaroni and cheese, which according to Nana would have made him like her even more. Mary was relieved when they pulled up at Judy's house. She thanked Nana and darted away from the car with her infant and baby stuff in tow.

Next she got to endure Judy's mom, Mrs. White ("No, call me Bitsy!" she said to Mary). Upon seeing Mary, she laughed and said, "You're a contradiction!" When Mary seemed confused, Bitsy said, "You've got a computerized baby but you're dressed like –"

"That's why we're going to the mall, Mom." Judy came to the door and welcomed Mary in.

"Just give me a few; I've got to straighten my hair," Bitsy said. She wore jeans and a hooded sweatshirt, her face in full makeup. Mary thought it was strange to be dressed like she was planning on doing work in the garden, but she'd noticed the same thing about how her mom dressed, who had left after dinner the other night, ominously saying she was "meeting a friend."

While Bitsy finished getting ready, Mary and Judy compared notes. Judy had gotten two hundred and fifty dollars and a cell phone. They called each other on their phones, talking just a few feet away from each other.

"Think what we could get if we pooled our money!" Mary said.

"We could buy a car!"

"Or eighty dresses!"

"Or a trip to Hollywood for all five of us!"

They giggled nervously, feeling the significance of so much money in their pockets.

"So you just bring this *phone* with you . . . *everywhere?*" Judy said into the phone while looking right at Mary.

Mary shrugged, "I guess so. I get calls even when I'm outside. It's not connected to anything. James called me on mine last night."

Judy hung up her phone excitedly. "He did? What did you talk about?"

"I didn't talk to him. I don't . . . like him anymore." Mary choked on the words, but tried to look convincing.

As a shocked Judy was about to ask more, her mom emerged, ready to take them shopping. In the car, Judy tried to get Mary to talk about James, but Mary gestured at Bitsy as if she didn't want to talk about it in front of Judy's mom, even though Bitsy was on her own little phone during the whole drive.

When they pulled up to the department store, they fell into a stunned silence. Where a single department store had once been, a megaplex of a building the size of seven or eight department stores now lay. How were they ever going to find Maxine, Bev, and Ann? Mary and Judy wished their friends had cell phones like they now had. A giant three-story movie theater anchored one end of the mall, with restaurants, specialty shops, and pet stores in between it and one of the large department stores at the other end.

"Where do you want to get let out?" Bitsy asked, lining up behind a row of cars. "Where are you meeting the others?"

"We said at the teen clothing section," Judy said, feeling foolish.

"Which one?"

Judy shrugged while Mary's shoulders sagged; the mayhem at the mall was just one more reminder that they were out of their element. A depressing fact in light of their resignation to "stay" in this strange future.

Judy made her mom drive around the entire complex once and they finally decided on an entrance that looked like it was one of the main ones.

"Unless you get a ride home, call me! I'll be at brunch with Roger!" Bitsy called before pulling away in her black sports car.

"Roger, Roger, Roger," huffed Judy. "I haven't even met this guy!"

"I haven't met my dad's fiancée, either," Mary commiserated.

"Golly, you're going to have a stepmother!" Judy realized.

Yet another layer of dread settled around Mary like a maddening fog.

They entered the mall through double layers of double glass doors and tried to take in the scene before them. Twelve-foot tall tropical trees sprouted out of pots the size of Judy's mother's car and lined a promenade that was three levels high. An arched glass ceiling let in the light, reflecting off of shiny surfaces that burned the girls' eyes. People bustled in every direction, many of them talking on phones and, strangely, not to each other. Canned music assaulted their ears and the smells of cinnamon buns, leather, and lemon cleaner were inescapable with every breath.

"It's not even Christmas," murmured Mary, overwhelmed by the "everyday" spectacle. How would they ever find the other girls, let alone find clothes that they liked enough to wear in public?

"What now?" Judy asked.

Just then, a voice echoed over the PA system of the entire mall. "Paging Judy White and Mary Donovan. Please come to the central concierge desk. Your party is waiting."

Judy and Mary glanced at each other and started laughing.

"To answer your question, we go to the concierge desk, wherever that is," Mary giggled. Her spirits started to lift ever so slightly.

After finding a large illumined sign that was a map of the mall, they made their way to the concierge desk where Ann, Maxine, and Bev were waiting. Mary flashed back to the day when they had all woken up in the future, when she came into social studies to see the girls looking as shaken and out of place as she must have looked and certainly felt.

Upon seeing each other, they greeted each other as if it had been twelve years, not twelve hours, since their last encounter.

"We've got to do this in a jiffy," Bev said. "Bob's picking me up so we can get there early for the game." She did not look like she intended to enjoy shopping.

"This place is enormous!" said Ann, dumbfounded.

In perfectly predictable fashion, it was Mary who said, "Let's come up with a plan."

The girls all moaned.

"What? Bev just said –"

"We love you." Maxine put her arm around Mary. "Let's just walk until we find something that looks good and we want to go in." Maxine knew that she still owed Mary an apology for accusing her of telling James their secret and so tried to be a little gentler than usual with her friend.

The girls agreed and started off. They didn't get far before they were seduced by giant chocolate chip cookies.

"Is it my imagination, or is everything bigger?" Ann said, staring at the cookie in her hand.

"And more expensive," said Mary. She couldn't get over the fact that what she had just spent on a cookie could have bought all the fabric and notions for a new dress.

Grace was quietly content with the motion of walking and everyone generously carried some of the baby's accoutrements to lighten Mary's load.

"Oh!" Bev and Maxine said at the same time, looking in opposite directions. Bev eyeballed a sports collector store, while Maxine was drawn to a bookstore.

Mary wanted to stick together. "Look at me. Am I interested in clothes? Jeans and T-shirts are all I wear unless I'm wearing my team uniform," Bev argued.

"And there's a book about Rosa Parks in there!" Maxine pointed. "She sat in the front of the bus in Montgomery, Alabama in December 1955. We just missed that . . . . " She referenced having time traveled six months too soon.

They agreed to meet up in a half hour at the food court, a vast sea of low-grade tables surrounded by vendors selling expensive but cheap-tasting fast food.

Judy brightened when she saw a clothing shop several stores down from where Bev and Maxine had peeled off. The three remaining girls went in, tentatively.

A sales girl with black spiky hair, a name tag that read "Sasha," and piercings all along the rims of both her ears approached, looked them up and down, and said, "Nice," in approving sincerity. "Vintage. I get it."

"Well, we're looking to . . . *modernize*," Judy said.

Within moments, the girls were loading Sasha down with anything they could find; she promised to "set up a room" for them.

When they had picked over the store indiscriminately, in a flurry of excitement, they made their way to the dressing rooms. Judy was in a state of euphoria, but even her enthusiasm wasn't enough to pull off many of the ensembles she chose. She posed for Mary and Ann in a sequined micro miniskirt and tall boots with a T-shirt that was so low-cut, she'd need to wear another shirt under it – except that it was too tight to fit a layer underneath. They vetoed that. She attempted an overly revealing tank top that displayed her undergarments on top and too-tight jeans that exposed her undergarments on the bottom. They shook their heads absolutely not. She tried on a patterned wraparound dress that was a little too wrap-around and got tangled up in it.

After exhausting many of her choices, Judy demanded that Mary and Ann strive to do better. Mary came out of her dressing room first in a black knee-length skirt and tailored jacket. "This isn't terrible," she said.

"Yes, it is. You look like you're forty!" Judy protested.

Ann came out in baggy cargo pants and an oversized hoodie; she looked like she was being eaten alive by a cotton monster. "No!" Judy laughed.

Round and round they went, laughing off most of the outfits they tried on until Mary found a ruffled blouse she liked, but needed a different size. She went to find the sales clerk while Ann and Judy debated the length of a skirt that Judy liked. In her dressing room, Mary's phone rang. Judy, proud to know how cell phones work, let herself into the dressing room and noticed James's name on the phone screen. "Oh!" she said and quickly answered the call.

"Mary?"

"This is Judy. I'm answering her cellular telephone," Judy said professionally.

"Is she with you then? Where are you? Her grandma said she's at the mall. I've been trying to track her down."

"Oh, sure. I'm with Mary. She'd love to see you." She told James the name of the clothing store, not buying Mary's earlier comment that she no longer liked him. "You'd better hurry, because we're headed for the food court in a few minutes."

Judy smiled at herself. If her arm were long enough, she would have patted herself on the back; it was obvious Mary still liked James and here was Judy being the perfect little match-maker, even though her own love life was on the outs.

"Who was that?" Ann asked, having a feeling she knew the answer.

"Don't say anything to Mary, but it was James. He's going to meet us –"

"What?" Only it wasn't Ann who screeched at Judy. It was Mary, who had just returned to overhear Judy's scheme.

Mary pushed past Judy to get to her dressing room and strip out of the store's clothing and get quickly into her own.

Ann and Judy were equally confused. "Mary." Judy reached out, but Mary slapped her hand away.

"I've got to get out of here," Mary said, tying her saddle shoes with fumbling fingers. This was not the time to see James, to try to explain – or not explain, as she was hoping would be the case. Either way, it came down to the fact that she wouldn't let her friends down again by being silly and selfish and going ape over James O'Grady. Mrs. Fairview knew something and if Mary was being tested for the sake of all the Fifties Chix, she wasn't going to fail.

She raced toward the front of the store with Ann and Judy at her heels.

The sales clerk called after them as an alarm sounded. Judy looked down, realizing she was still in clothes she had yet to decide on and purchase, as did Ann.

"Sorry!" they both cried and jumped back into the store.

"It wasn't you who set it off," Sasha said as a security officer dashed toward them. She pointed him toward Mary, already twenty feet out of the store, and a moment later, he returned with Mary's arm clenched in his beefy fist. She struggled to get out of his grip, flailing. Her glasses slipped off and her hair started to fall out of its tidy ponytail.

"I didn't do anything! Let me go!"

Sasha accompanied Mary and the security officer to the back of the store, where she discovered a close-fitting black skirt underneath Mary's circle skirt. "I didn't know!" Mary wailed. "I don't even *like* that skirt!" While the security guard pelted her with accusations, Judy and Ann changed into their clothes and rushed back to Mary's side to advocate for her innocence.

"You two can go," the security guard indicated to Judy and Ann. "But *you're* coming with me for questioning," he said pointedly to Mary.

Even as the security guard marched her down the center of the mall, Ann and Judy followed faithfully. They were both shaken and scared, but knew that Mary was more so. They turned and went down an inconspicuous hallway that led to a cold, bland room. The guard sat Mary down on a metal folding chair and proceeded to get out some paperwork, asking her for her name, parents' names, address, and other details. When she was asked about her birthday, she paused and summoned up the year she had given James. "January 13, 1995." She had hardly faltered before lying about her birth year and Judy and Ann looked impressed.

After more paperwork, more questions, a stern lecture, and a phone call about to be made to her mother, Mary realized that she should drop the argumentative bit and try on a little remorse for size. She apologized sincerely, maintaining it was a mistake and that it would certainly never happen again.

Finally, a little exhausted from dealing with this himself, and because his radio was going off every thirty seconds about other emergencies, the security guard excused Mary with an admonition and the mandate to not visit that store again for a long while. That was easy to agree to. Mary was relieved – and confounded by her dumb luck – that a call wasn't made home. She was devolving into a regular criminal: being sent to the office, breaking into Mrs. F's apartment and stealing her lipstick, and now being hauled in for suspected shoplifting.

Somewhat bedraggled, the trio headed for the food court, wondering if their friends would even still be waiting for them.

"This is why everyone should have a cellular telephone," Judy insisted.

This registered something with Mary. "The baby!" she gasped, grabbing Judy and Ann, who were on either side of her. Her stomach flip-flopped. How could she have forgotten? When was the last time she had even seen that blasted thing? Only now, especially now, she couldn't think of it as a "thing" – at the very least, it was an expensive piece of machinery that she couldn't afford to replace and it would cost her her grade; at most, she had become attached to it – to *her*.

The girls, once again sidetracked from the food court, bolted back to the clothing store. Ann and Judy told Mary to wait outside, but came out a few moments later empty-handed. Sasha had gone home for the day and the current sales clerk didn't know anything about a baby, real or computerized.

The only thing they could think to do was return to the security guard's dreadful office and report a kidnapping.

15

It's not You, it's Her

After filling out yet more paperwork, Mary gave the pen back to the security guard. He looked at her meaningfully and said, "Not so fun when someone steals from you, is it?" As her eyes filled with tears, he scrambled to take it back. "We'll find your . . . doll. . . . ."

"She's not a *doll*, she's a computerized –"

Her cell phone rang, cutting off her rising panic, until she saw who it was. She started to put the phone away, but Judy snatched it from her. "Oh, for goodness' sake. Give me that!" She opened the phone and answered it.

"Hi, James, this is Judy again."

"I'm not here!" Mary whispered loudly. Ann rolled her eyes. *Oh, brother.* At least she had James O'Grady calling her; she didn't have to act like it was the worst thing in the world!

"*What?*" Judy squealed. "We're coming right now!"

Judy hung up the phone, shoving it into Mary's hand and grabbing the paperwork back from the security guard. "What are you –?" Mary asked.

"James has Grace! He's at the food court. Let's go!"

Mary's head swam. Not only was she going to have to face James, but she owed him yet another favor. The last thing she needed was to be further indebted to him!

Mary and Ann were reluctant, but Judy seized their wrists and pulled them forward.

A moment later, they rounded the corner by the food court and spotted James standing next to Bev, Maxine, and Bob, who were sitting at a small metal table. On top of the table was Grace in her carrier, not making a peep. Now Judy, upon seeing Bob, was as reluctant as her two friends and slowed to half-time.

"There you are!" Bev called out. "Bob is here to take me to the game! We're going to be late!"

"Sorry," Mary said. "It's a long story." She avoided eye contact with James. It was like trying to not look directly at the sun when it's the only thing on the horizon giving light to the whole universe. Mary inspected Grace, muttering a "thanks" in his direction.

James explained how he had gone to the clothing boutique to meet them and heard Grace crying in the dressing room. He'd told the sales clerk, Sasha, that he knew who the baby belonged to, describing Mary, and promised to bring it to her. Sasha had been just getting off work, so she'd been happy for someone else to deal with the problem.

Judy, nervous, burst out, "Mary got arrested."

"Judy!" Mary exclaimed.

"What happened?" Maxine asked.

"I'm sure there's a great story here, but we gotta jam. If we're late, Coach won't let us play," Bob said, tugging on Bev. "Bye, guys. See ya, Judy."

Judy blushed at being singled out. Mary wished she could go with Bev and Bob to escape, but they were going directly to the field.

"See you at the game," Maxine assured them.

"Well, it's later than I thought; we'd better get going," Mary said, collecting the various baby things that her friends had been carrying for her.

"Mary, can I talk to you for a minute?" James said. He seemed miffed.

"We're running late. Maybe another time?"

Judy piped up, "We're getting a sandwich, aren't we, girls? You two go ahead and talk; we'll be back in a few minutes." And before Mary could say a thing in response, Maxine, Ann, and Judy drifted away. Mary looked after them longingly.

James asked what was going on. Mary busied herself looking at Grace's diaper.

He asked again, being, he felt, remarkably patient. "Is this about Mrs. Fairview?" She shook her head no. "Is this about the poem?"

"What poem?" she asked. He had her attention now.

"Never mind. Can you just tell me what I did wrong?"

Finally, Mary mustered all her courage. She still couldn't look him in the eye, or she would never get the words out. "I don't want to see you any more. I really appreciate your help and everything, but I think there's been a misunderstanding. And I need to spend more time with my friends."

He lowered his voice, but because it was his voice, she could still easily hear him over the bustle of the mall and the piped-in music. "I thought I was a friend. Is it because of the time-travel thing? I'll stop bugging you about it. Is it something else, Mary?"

"I just can't talk about any of it, especially to you!" Mary snapped. James looked like he'd been slapped in the face and Mary felt like she'd been punched in the stomach. She wanted to immediately take it back, but she said nothing.

"Gotcha," James said coldly. "You're welcome, by the way, for rescuing your 'baby'." He pulled his keys out of his pocket, and for lack of something better to do, twirled them around his finger. "Well, see ya. Oh, I mean, I *won't* see you. Apparently."

He stalked off, then paused and turned to look back at her. She was facing the other way. He wanted to say something along the lines of "take care" or "if you change your mind . . ." but the words lodged in his throat and he turned back around and left.

When Ann, Maxine, and Judy returned, Mary hadn't moved, but tears were sliding down her face, one after the other. In an instant, her friends' arms were around her and she had the distant thought, *It's already working.*

"Does all this have anything to do with me?" Ann whispered, feeling guilty for some of the thoughts she'd had about Mary and seeing her hurt now.

"It has to do with all of you. From now on, I'm going to be a better friend, I promise."

Ann and Judy went in for another hug. No matter what had transpired between all of them, they didn't want to see their friend heartbroken. No one deserved that kind of agony.

Row finished up the watering in the window boxes. It would be a blistering day, and the first of many. There was nothing quite like a midwest summer to keep you on your toes in the garden. Her trusty begonias, petunias, and Black-eyed Susans always bloomed faithfully, but it was the delicate flowers that took the most care and were the most rewarding when they bloomed. And wasn't that the case in life, too? The hardy folks were reliable, but not nearly as interesting. It was the ones who required extra care and attentiveness who were most fascinating when they blossomed into their own.

Her thought was on her friend May, of course. May was delicate and high-maintenance without knowing it. That's why Row had spent a lifetime protecting her, cheering her on, nurturing her; because when May shined there was nothing quite as lovely in the world. How she could explain that to May was a mystery. How do you tell a friend that you lied to her for fifty-five years for her own protection? *Well, you don't,* Row figured. *You keep protecting her.*

She loved Em as well, of course, but Emily Jackson had a genuine independent streak and knew how to get things done; there was nothing delicate about Em unless the role called for it. But Em's jumping ship was a weakness in Row's eyes, a lack of courage. At least May was sticking with it. Row often marveled that things had turned out the way they had; life was never short on surprises, that was for sure.

Oh, boy.

Row scrounged through her little handbag for a light.

The groom stood slumped at the street corner and everyone was clustered around him, smothering the poor guy. Especially his mother, who had pushed so hard for this day to be perfect. But perfect for whom? And now, as usual, Row was left to clean up the mess.

She approached him directly and pulled him away from the crowd, purposely avoiding fake cheer or too much sympathy.

"Light?" she said.

He looked up, nodded, and pulled a cigarette out. "She's always trying to get me to quit," he said.

"Nasty habit," Row agreed. Reggie took a deep puff, then offered the cigarette to her. "No, thanks," Row said. "She did get me to quit."

He snorted something close to a laugh and stamped the butt out. "What now?" he asked. He looked at his fiancée's best friend. Row's hair was in smooth tidy blonde curls that looked like polished gold. She carried herself with confidence and pep and knew just how to handle people; she was an open book. He should have brought her home to his mother; everything would have been a lot simpler. If only he had fallen for Rowena Nolan; but he hadn't. He had fallen for Marion Boggs.

"You tell me," Row said, shielding her eyes from the glaring sun. She looked at the trees shimmying in the breeze and a flock of tiny birds gathered on a low branch like a row of tiny black fists. "Nice day for a wedding," she noted.

"Was it me?" he asked. For a fleeting second his guard was down and instead of being the dashing prince, he looked like a hurt young boy.

Row pulled her gloves off and fanned herself with them. Behind her in the church, there was a flurry of activity as people scattered away and re-gathered to gossip and speculate. *"It wasn't you, Reggie. It's all her."*

"Somehow that doesn't comfort me, sweetheart." He was wishing he hadn't stamped out that cigarette. His hair felt hot in the sun, like the VO5 dressing cream was going to slide right off, and his nerves were frayed.

Row sighed. Why did she have to do everything? *"Do you still love her, sport?"*

"Of course!" He looked at her sharply.

"Then go get her and marry her the way she wants to be married."

"Where will I find her?"

"One guess."

He paused for only the briefest second. *"The ridge property!"*

"I'll get the priest, you bring the car around." Row smiled.

Reggie darted off, then stopped and ran back to Row, kissing her on the cheek. *"Thank you. You're like a sister to May and that makes you my sister, too."*

Now Row's bravado faltered. She thought of the brothers she had lost in the war ten years before. She blushed and fumbled over her words. *"Oh, golly, Reggie. Thank you . . . ."*

As she dashed into the church to find the minister, she sighed to herself, *"Always the sister, never the bride."*

Row stood up straight, stretching and brushing the soil from her knees. Time had a way of flying when she worked in the garden. Hours slipped by without notice. It tended to cause a strange mixture of satisfaction and panic; it was nice to escape, but life was already blowing by her with increasing speed and it made her uneasy. The frailty and changeableness of time were unnerving.

She had cleared out the faded irises and other spring bulbs and cleaned out underneath the rhodies and azaleas; she had even planted and staked the baby tomatoes. She was already dreaming of tomato sandwiches with fresh basil from her kitchen flower box.

James rounded the corner then.

"Thought you weren't coming today," Aunt Row said. "Isn't there a game or something you were going to, Jimmy?"

"Yeah, but I don't wanna go. Besides, look at all the work that needs to be done around here." He glanced around, not actually seeing a lot that needed to be done, thanks to Aunt Row's determined efforts and his generous help over the last several months.

"Tell Aunt Row," she sighed, seeing the distress plain on his face.

Without hesitating, James jumped right in. If it was anyone in the world he could talk to, it was Aunt Row. "It's Mary. I thought getting her to talk to Mrs. F would make everything better, but it's worse. All of a sudden she wants nothing to do with me. I don't know what it is!"

"I can tell you this much: it's not you, it's her," Aunt Row said for what felt like the millionth time in her life. "And by her, I mean *her*." She hooked her thumb toward Mrs. F's apartment. "I'll talk to her."

"You think it was something Mrs. F said to Mary?"

"Dollars-to-dumplings." Aunt Row repeated one of her favorite sayings. "You go to the game and try to enjoy yourself. Don't you worry about Mary; she's crazy about you. Now, get. There's nothing for a young strapping handsome man like yourself to do around here, anyway. Your looks are wasted on me; I already love you."

James blushed. "Thanks, Aunt Row. I love you, too." He plucked a twig from her hair and gave her a hug.

16

Love isn't a Game

Bev's heart pounded in her chest and she wondered if everyone else could see it. There was nothing quite like a big game and being in the presence of Conrad Marshall to get her blood pumping. She had gotten a grip and could now make a play without being distracted by the dreamy center fielder, but her new challenge was not being sidetracked by what was going on in the stands.

Before leaving the mall, Judy had blurted something about Mary being arrested (which sounded nothing like Mary, but then again, Mary hadn't been herself for a while now. Love, like baseball playoff games, pushed you to do outrageous things). As she searched the bleachers, Bev noted that Mary was absent, as were Bev's parents. Judy was in attendance, but she looked far from her regular self in a new getup from the mall and a sour-puss expression. Bev hadn't heard her cheer even once. The funny thing was, Judy was dressed like the girls from school while the girls from school were busy trying to look like Judy.

With the exception of Diane Dunkelman, who seemed extra perky in the stands. Maxine watched dutifully, but she was there just as much for her cousin Conrad.

Then there was Gary, the only family member who cared enough to show up (besides Bob, of course, who didn't have a choice as team pitcher); and Gary seemed more concerned with Ann's well-being than with his little sister's performance on the field. Maybe they had already forgotten what an achievement it was for a girl to be playing with the boys' varsity team. And, for crying out loud, hadn't anyone seen her diving catch of that line drive in the second inning that resulted in a double play?

Yes. Conrad had.

She glanced back at him in center field. He was hunkered down and focused on the hitter at the plate, which reminded her to focus. She couldn't get caught up in all this drama; she had a game to win.

The count was three and two and Bob, pitching, wound up. A crack of the bat sent the ball sailing, another line drive up the middle; Bev made her move to intersect it, but realized that the ball hadn't made it all the way to her. Instead there was a nasty thump and Bob crumpled into a heap. Without wasting a moment to think, Bev rushed to her brother. Only a split second later, Coach and the catcher, Marsallis, had joined her. The rest of the team soon circled around. There had been a collective groan from the stands, and now an anxious silence prevailed as Bob remained immobile on the ground. Coach had his hands full trying to calm Beverly, never mind trying to rouse his star pitcher.

"Marshall." Coach said only one word pointedly and Conrad understood. He took Bev gently by the arm and pulled her away from the crowd. Conrad spoke in quiet, soothing tones trying to reassure her, but just this once, her attention lay elsewhere than on him. After what felt like an eternity, Bob stirred and responded to questions. Bev was supremely relieved for Bob and also infuriated that her parents where nowhere to be found when her brother needed them. With help, Bob stood and hobbled toward the dugout. The crowd cheered.

Gary made his way down from the grandstand, with Judy and Diane close behind.

"Swell. You *are* here," sneered Bev at her other brother. He looked confusedly at her, but she had no patience to explain it to him at the moment.

"Jenkins Part Two, you up for some pitching?" Coach asked. Although he wasn't asking, of course, he was telling. "Warm up, then get us out of this inning."

"Where's Judy?" mumbled Bob.

Everyone looked at Bob in confusion . . . except for Judy, who was beaming; and Diane, who was scowling. "You mean Bev," corrected Bev.

"Judy," Bob repeated.

"Hi, Bob," Judy said with cautious pleasure. Diane Dunkelman folded her arms tight across her chest and flicked her head in disdain.

Coach told Bev not to worry, Bob was just a little rattled, and encouraged her to focus and get ready to pitch.

Once on the mound, Bev cleared her mind and made room for nothing but throwing, catching, and winning. And win she did, beating the Crusaders handily 8-3. Victory was always sweet; but this one left a little to be desired with an injured brother and the absence of certain friends and family. Conrad must have known how she felt because while everyone else was cheering that they were advancing to the regional quarterfinals, he continued to talk to her in a subdued voice.

Row rapped on May's front door. It was courtesy; she could have just walked in, even if the door was locked, since as the landlady she had a key. In fact, she walked in anyway because May didn't answer.

"I was eating," May said, annoyed. She sat at the small dinette in the back of her apartment. Row was glad to see that at least the windows were open and a hot breeze was circulating through the place. The first step out of a funk is to let the light in.

"You do seem awfully busy," Row said. Then, "I brought this for you." She slid a thick leather photo album next to May's sandwich plate.

May caressed to top of the book with one finger and then went back to her sandwich. She tried the direct route: "Why?"

"Just cleaning out over at my place. I'm not a storage unit, you know, and I gotta make some space for my own stuff."

May looked at her and then through the front window at Row's huge estate. Where she lived alone. There was certainly no shortage of space there.

Row knew May would argue along these lines and preempted her by saying, "I don't want poor Jimmy or his mom or cousins to have to sort through all my things when I die. I'm trying to make it easy on them, okay?"

"You'll never die," retorted May in a tone that came out more bitter than she had intended.

Now Row looked at her and they both giggled.

"I'm sorry," May said, her voice softening. "It's just that I know why you brought this. You think I'll look through it, get all sentimental, reconcile with Reggie, be so softened by it all that I'll go easy on those girls, and we'll all live happily ever after."

"You said it, not me."

"It doesn't work that way," sighed May.

"You don't want to try?" Row sat across from her friend at the small, tidy kitchenette. Memories of their single days – May's single days – washed over Row. This apartment, where May had been living when she got engaged to Reggie; the garage below which once upon a time – Row knew firsthand – had been a barn for horses and mules; in fact, every nook and cranny of the house and property had layers and generations of stories. Some of them unbearable to relive, even as memories. Some of them sweet and simple, like when Row dropped by during the wee hours when May was grading papers and they'd get to talking and stay up all night.

"Say, why doesn't that dumb bird fly out?" Row asked suddenly looking at Ike, who sat contentedly on his branch in the kitchen next to an open window.

May shrugged. "Guess he thinks he's in a cage."

Row stared outside for a long moment and then said quietly, "That's the worst kind of cage, isn't it? The one that exists only in our imagination."

"How would you feel if you found out your marriage was a lie?" May asked.

"His love for you was never a lie. And people get married for all kinds of reasons."

"Oh, Row. Reggie didn't know what he was asking for, did he? Not really."

"Nope," agreed Row. "He did ask for *you*, though." She smiled.

And after a long moment, May's lips curled up at the corners ever so slightly, too.

Dear Diary, December 19, 1954

This afternoon was the parish Christmas party. I wore a red sweater Nana knitted and my snow boots...even though it's not snowing! I wore them in hopes that we will have a white Christmas; that way, it will be pretty outside AND my father will be snowed in. . . or out, as the case may be. We haven't seen him in a year. I guess because it's Christmas, he thinks he should see us. But it just makes me sad. Last year, he brought me a pair of mittens and a muffler; I had to give them to Patty and Maggie because they were too small for me. That's what happens when you're not around...your kids grow up and you don't even know it.

I'm not entirely sad; I met a dreamy boy tonight. His name is James O'Grady and he goes to my school. Well. . . I didn't exactly meet him – he doesn't know I exist. But after singing some Christmas carols, we went to the cafeteria for a potluck (you've never seen so much food!). I made my macaroni and cheese, Nana made a Christmas stollen, and Mom made green bean casserole. We were all feeling swell after all those cheerful carols. Even the kids were behaving themselves. I had seen James during the caroling. He was actually singing, not like the other boys who looked like they couldn't be bothered (why do they even come, I ask you?). James has this beautiful red hair and not like mine, which is too orange. His is a deep rich auburn. Anyway, we all stood in line for the food and he was helping some blond lady on crutches. She looked too young to be his mom;

maybe she was his aunt. He picked out all her food for her and I heard him say he couldn't wait to try the macaroni and cheese, which is what I made!! I watched him get her settled in at a big round table (I wished we could have sat there, too, but Mom and Nana already had folks for us to eat with). Then another lady at the table asked James to get her something; he brought it to her and another lady asked for a spoon. He must have gone back and forth four times! By the time he went to get his own food, the mac and cheese was gone and the only thing left was fruitcake and cookies with nuts! But, Diary, he didn't complain. And I watched when he would think no one was looking and he didn't even make a face or look sad. I wished I could be that kind. I resolved then and there that I was going to be more gracious to my friends and family. I guess that includes my father, then. Well, if James O'Grady can help me forgive my father, he is one special boy indeed.

Off to finish sewing my Christmas presents before bed. . . matching PJs for the whole family!

Always,
Mary

P.S. I put my diary under my pillow, but when I went to write in it tonight, I found it under my bed...is someone reading my diary?? I'm going to find a much better hiding place!

Dear Diary,   Dec. 19, 1954

I had the best day with Susan today. I can't
believe there are only 8 days before she splits. She
keeps telling me there's a chance the military will
move them back soon, but we know how that goes.
We went ice skating at Forest Park and then
when we were too frozen to move, we saw "White
Christmas" and thawed out with lots of hot popcorn. Bing Crosby has the dreamiest voice...and he
has those sweet sad eyes that remind me of Bob
Jenkins. Susan and I tried to decide who was
who in the movie and we decided that I am Rose-
mary Clooney ("Betty") because she ends up with
Bing and Susan is Vera-Ellen ("Judy," isn't that
a kick?) who ends up with Danny Kaye. That
works out perfectly because Susan is a wonderful
dancer! Maybe we can travel together like "Betty
and Judy" someday & take our show on the road!
Tomorrow is one more day with each other...and
guess what? We're going to see "White Christmas" again because it's Christmas vacation! (I
hope we really do get a white Christmas, it would
be dreamy. It would cheer me up because Christmas without Daddy is so sad.) We'll also go by
Jenkins Hardware because Bob is working over
the holidays. Did I ever mention that his sister
Bev is in my class at school? I should become
tight with her so I can hang around Bob!

Good night and Merry Christmas,
 Judy White aka Judy Jenkins

Sunday - December 19, 1954

I don't know why Christmas makes me sad. I think it's because we sing all these spirituals in church about the baby Jesus and how he was born so we can be free. I always wonder who the "we" is? It's been almost two thousand years, how much longer do we have to wait? We are celebrating Christmas on Wednesday night because Mama and Daddy both have to work on Christmas. Do their bosses not think that they have a family, too? White folks make me so mad! Mama says the only way to be free is to love and that's what our Lord and Savior told us. Well, she is loving her way right out of a proper family Christmas, unless she thinks the Johnsons are her family. At least Melba is home for break from college. We'll go to Uncle TJ's and cousin Conrad's for Christmas and have roast pork. Some other folks from church will be there and we'll sing Christmas songs and I'll try not to cry when I think of what they did to Jesus at the end of his life...and what they're doing to us now.

Maxine

Pops won't let me work at the hardware store! He says if I want money, just ask him, but "retail during the holidays isn't a proper place for a lady"! I'm bored out of my mind. It's too cold to go out for a catch, not that there's anyone to play with because they're all at the store. Mom asked if I wanted to learn to crochet. I looked at her like she had cooties! This is the longest Christmas break of my life. I can't wait to get back to school and back to training. It's between me and Diane Dunkelman for team captain of the softball team come spring. I can tell you who it WON'T be . . . Diane Dunkelman.
-Bev

Dear Irina,   19 December 1954

I can imagine your first night of Hanukkah was sad and beautiful with snow on the ground. Here, it is just cold and bleak. There is so little inspiration when the world seems blanched of color; I try to find the color in the gray, but it is hard. As you well know, shadows have no color.

Tonight, we placed the first candle and sang songs and ate till we were stuffed, latkes and more sufganiyot then a person should be allowed, especially when so many go hungry in the world. I'm too old to play dreidel, but Alex still gets a kick out of it, so it is fun. When Tatty tested us on our knowledge of Hanukkah, Alex did better than I did (not surprising since it is less than a year until his Bar Mitzvah and he has been studying hard!). In my last letter, I told you that I was going to paint a little canvas for each member of my family. They all liked them very much! I got a tube of cobalt oil paint from my parents. It is the most expensive color and I love it! It is the color of the May evening sky . . . I can't wait until it is May and the flowers are blooming and there will be so much to paint, I won't be able to choose! I also received from them a cool hat that looks like a gondolier in Venice would wear! Perhaps I'll mail you a photograph.

Fortunately, Mama got time off for Sukkot in October, but I think they are trying to make up for it this week. With Christmas coming, she will be working late every night which means we will be lighting the candles at sundown without her. And . . . every year, they still ask her to prepare the Christmas ham!! And every year she refuses.

Happy Festival of Lights, my dear cousin. I hope that you have much to celebrate.

   —Ann

Mary closed her diary. Why was she torturing herself reading and re-reading her entry about the first time she saw James? Because she was hoping there was an answer there, a way to show Mrs. F and her friends – no, herself – that he was a good boy and he made her a better person. But the only way to show that wasn't by obsessing over her past diary entries; it was to prove it, like she did that Christmas with her dad.

And like that Christmas with her dad, she'd get her chance to be gracious tonight: Dad was picking her up for dinner so she could meet his fiancée.

17

Group Think

Ann walked to where she remembered Aunt Row's house was and every step felt like she was treading on nails. She thought of her parents leaving Belgrade, leaving their family and everything they knew; she could only imagine what it would have been like for them, the tears shed, the goodbyes, even the angry silences on the part of those who didn't understand why they were leaving and felt betrayed. Her parents had done it all on faith in a better future for the children they didn't even have yet. It was a great sacrifice for their future family. Ann searched her mind, but couldn't come up with anything she'd ever had to sacrifice. Hadn't her parents raised her to be better than that? To live for something beyond just herself?

She had always been introspective, but at what expense? She thought of James, then the reason she was going to see Mrs. Fairview. Well, James and Mary, of course. James had intrigued Ann and she liked that he had a gentle artistic side; he reminded her of her dad. But she didn't have any shared experiences with him (apart from art class), while Mary did. She had watched Mary try to hide and then apologize for her feelings for James and, as of yesterday, try to pretend she had no feelings for him. Ann had made no similar effort. Ann wondered if the poem that had intrigued her so in *The Invisible Truth* had been written by James about her and Mary. Maybe it was a stretch – or even wishful thinking that he harbored any feelings for Ann at all – but if there was any chance that he liked *both* of them . . . .

Ann didn't know quite what to do and so found herself seeking out Mrs. Fairview. It seemed like a long shot, and she hadn't the foggiest idea what would be accomplished by a conversation with Mrs. F about it, but she felt impelled to try.

She arrived at Aunt Row's house and debated going to her front door first. But Ann knew she would only be procrastinating, delaying facing Mrs. Fairview face to face. As she approached Mrs. F's apartment, she allowed herself to breathe deeply and relaxed her shoulders before knocking on the door.

Mrs. Fairview opened the door almost immediately. She didn't seem surprised to see Ann. Ann wasn't prepared to feel so overwhelmed with relief at the sight of her teacher, on whom she had been convinced so much relied.

"Anna. Please join us," Mrs. Fairview said wryly.

It wasn't until she stepped inside that she understood Mrs. Fairview's reaction. There on a beige sofa Maxine and Judy sat side by side, looking somewhat sheepish.

"Oh," was all Ann could muster.

"I'd offer some lemonade, but I might as well wait until everyone gets here," said Mrs. F.

"I didn't know – " Ann started.

"They didn't either. Judy came and Maxine showed up shortly thereafter," Mrs. F explained.

"Hiya," Judy said and Maxine waved hello.

Ann sat in a wooden chair adjacent to the sofa and had barely crossed her legs when there was a knock at the door. She, Maxine, and Judy looked at each other in faint wonder. A large gray bird that Ann hadn't noticed when she walked in squawked, "I like Ike!"

Mrs. F opened the door and welcomed Beverly in.

"Hey, Mrs. F, I just . . . oh," Beverly said upon seeing her three best friends.

"I swear we didn't plan this," Judy said. She was glad it turned out the way it had; she had been nervous at the prospect of facing Mrs. F alone.

Mrs. Fairview was sure they hadn't planned it either; but she would not have been surprised if Row had. She fetched the two kitchen chairs and brought them the short distance into the living area. Bev took a seat and then Mrs. F asked who would like lemonade, knowing intuitively that Mary would not be joining them.

Mrs. F was pleased that Maxine spoke first. Maxine, the bright and lovely young woman who had so much to say, but often hadn't said it just because of the color of her skin. "We have a lot of questions, but if these gals are anything like me, they came first and foremost because of Mary."

The others nodded in agreement.

"She told you about our get-together yesterday?" Mrs. F said, passing a plate of cookies. She may have been an old lady living alone (for the moment, at least), but she'd always have a stash of cookies for guests.

They nodded again. "She's been acting kooky ever since . . . well, kookier than usual . . ." Bev said.

Mrs. F wrung her hands nervously. She hadn't meant to make things worse for Mary. "Does it have anything to do with what I said about James O'Grady?"

"She didn't tell us you said anything about James," Judy said. A light flickered on in each of the girls; Mary had been so nutsville in reviling James all of a sudden – was it because of something Mrs. Fairview had said to her?

"James is a fine young man," Mrs. F said, "but – "

"But what?" piped up Ann.

"She was distracted by his attention," Mrs. F said, expecting the girls to get her meaning and agree. They didn't respond, waiting for her to continue. After a pause, she added, "You've all been put in a very – uh, *delicate* situation, I understand that; but you need to work together as friends, not go off in your own directions with your own plans." Mrs. Fairview desperately wanted them to understand. She'd had to choose between two lives: a traditional and happy life with the man of her dreams, and a life of adventure and wonder traveling to other eras. And she was struggling with the one she'd chosen. It was not going to be any different for them – or, specifically, Mary. Mary may as well make some hard choices about James now instead of having to do it down the road. If only they could understand that she, Mrs. Fairview, was doing this out of love.

"By delicate situation, I assume you mean time travel?" Bev asked boldly.

"Well, yes and no. It's not exactly time travel. I don't totally understand it myself; it's more of an indefinite glimpse at a parallel universe . . . but no matter what, the point is you need to work together."

The girls had been patiently suppressing their mounting questions for far too long, and Mrs. F knew she was opening a can of worms by saying as much as she had. Her intention was to help Mary focus, and she felt sure that the girls would have agreed with her. There was an outburst of inquiry that erupted from the girls at the same time:

"You told Mary not to like James anymore?"

"You made us time travel?"

"You left us alone to try to figure this out?"

"Does 'glimpse' mean we're going back soon?"

Even Ike joined in, "Reggie watch!"

Mrs. F curiously responded to Ike first with an adamant "Hush, Ike!" and then a defensive, "First of all, I didn't tell Mary *not* to like James – "

"Because you can't tell someone not to like a boy," Judy burst out passionately. The other girls looked at her meaningfully to zip it while Mrs. F was finally on the brink of spilling the beans. Judy immediately shut up.

"– I simply suggested that she focus on her friends," Mrs. F continued. "And no, I didn't *make* you time travel . . . exactly . . . I hardly know more than you do. And you are not alone . . . . " She started to say, "I'm here to help you," but realized that, of course, she hadn't been there for them at all. Instead, she said, "Oh, dear," and her eyes misted over. She had been going about this all wrong. Row had been right. Here she was trying to coerce these girls into turning to each other for help, and she herself didn't heed her own conviction by trusting her own friends: Row, or . . . Reggie. She hadn't even given him the opportunity to explain himself.

The girls stared at Mrs. F in a stunned silence. Seeing their teacher in a state of ambivalence was foreign. Wasn't she supposed to be the strong one with all the answers? Even if she didn't have *all* the answers, just *some* was more than they had.

"You are just as beautiful as Tom described," raved Tiffani.

Mary hadn't expected the kind introduction to her future stepmother. She blushed and her father beamed.

"I told you," he said to Tiffani while he squeezed Mary's hand.

Mary and her dad had picked up Tiffani from her apartment and Mary had been nearly incapacitated by nerves on the ride over. She would rather have met her dad's new wife on his wedding day, wished them best wishes, and then cut them both out. But, sadly, instead she was cutting *other* people out of her life, people she wanted in it . . . her throat got dry in that I'm-about-to-cry kind of way, so she quickly squelched any thoughts of James O'Grady.

Mary was also feeling vulnerable without Grace present to act as a buffer. Her mother and Nana had insisted she leave the mechanical infant at home, assuring her that they would explain to her teacher the circumstances if needed when the computer showed that Mary had been "neglectful" on Saturday night. Mary was unreasonable about the idea of leaving the baby, convinced – no matter how foolish the notion was – that Grace "needed" her or would "miss" her.

Adding to this, her mom had told Mary, in an attempt to make her feel better, that she herself had a date and didn't wish Mary's dad any ill will in moving forward. She told Mary not to think that Mary was being disloyal by accepting her father's fiancée into their family. Mary's head swam as she wondered how her mother's commentary was supposed to be comforting.

And now, in the presence of lovely Tiffani (with whom Mary had decided she would find fault on her own, with or without her mother's blessing), Mary was even more confused. Tiffani seemed genuine, down-to-earth, and practical, but still sunny. A hard combination to come by, and Mary's dad seemed to know it.

Glancing at Mary's "vintage" summer skirt, Tiffani said, "Tom, you know what would be fun? Let's take Mary to that great little fifties diner." Then she smiled broadly at Mary. Great. To make things worse, Tiffani wasn't judging Mary for dressing the way she did, but validating it. Tiffani was making it difficult for Mary to dislike her.

Mary saw a new side of her dad, too, one that the more it appeared, the more she realized it was vaguely familiar. She could recall moments before the arrival of Maggie, Patty, and Danny when her dad could have been considered light-hearted. Maybe she could somehow blame Tiffani for this, but she couldn't think how.

At the diner, to which Mary vowed to bring her girlfriends, she continued to relax despite her best efforts to be on guard. Munching on a burger and fries and gulping down a root beer float (in honor of Judy), she chatted with Tiffani and her father, forgetting herself for a few heavenly moments. The white and black checkerboard floor, pastel-colored walls, red vinyl bar seats, metal-rimmed table and chairs, and the walls lined with pictures of James Dean, Marilyn Monroe, and many other of Judy's favorites put Mary at ease. She was vaguely aware that the decor was just a gimmick, but she chose to go along with it. She even ignored the artifice of the gum-chomping waitress who kept obnoxiously referring to Mary as "doll."

Tiffani asked about Mary's friends and Mary told her a little about each of her four friends; her dad seemed interested and she realized he'd never asked about them and consequently knew nothing about them. Tiffani then asked good-naturedly if there was a boy Mary liked.

Mary's dad laughed uncomfortably and said, "Do I even want to know?"

Mary hoped to avoid the question just as much as her dad, but once again, the rosy pigment in her blushing cheeks betrayed her, answering the question involuntarily.

Mary didn't know how it happened, but with a few strategic questions on Tiffani's part, Mary was revealing that she had to choose between her friends and the boy she liked.

"Hm. That doesn't make sense. Isn't *he* a friend?"

Mary thought about it and nodded yes.

"Are your girlfriend 'friends'?"

She nodded yes again.

"They don't sound like friends if they asked you to stop liking him."

"Oh, they didn't," Mary clarified. "It's just that . . . ." She felt like it was too complicated to go into without mentioning that oh, by the way, she had time-traveled.

"Well, I say you can never have too many friends. You should never have to choose."

And that's where Mary found Tiffani's fatal flaw: Tiffani over-simplified everything and she would never understand Mary's plight! Mary fixated on Tiffani's words, hoping that they would twist and expand and show Tiffani's true nature as a real turkey, but the more Mary thought about it, the more it actually made sense.

18

New Normal

Dear Diary,   May 22nd

Tonight I met Dad's fiancée. I kept expecting it to be horrible, for her to be horrible, but she wasn't that bad. Chalk up another thing that doesn't go the way I expected. But if you can believe it, I have even bigger news than that. This morning I went to the mall and got arrested!

Oh, drat it all. Nana is calling me downstairs for something. I'll be right back to finish!

Dear Diary,   May 22

I have so much to tell you, I don't know
where to start. Oh! Of course I do. With
Bob.
Diane Dunkelman said he thinks of me as a
little sister? the worst, right? Only he got
clunked in the head at his baseball game and
in his delirium he asked for ME. NOT Diane
or even Bev, but for me. Twice. I saw in
that moment that Bev was right: what
Diane had told me, that girls are making fun
of us, is just a lie because she is jealous.
Realizing that when I heard Bob say my
name? Well, that made up for everything,
even a terrible morning at the mall where
Mary accidentally stole a skirt. Honestly, it
was an accident, she didn't even like the
skirt. After the game, being so happy about
Bob and all, I got up my nerve to go talk to
Mrs. Fairview about Mary. See, I know
that Mary likes James a whole lot, but she
was walking around suddenly saying she
didn't like him anymore. Well, not
"suddenly"...only after she talked to Mrs. F!

I think if Mary likes James then that's cool with me and it should be cool with everyone else. I know Ann likes James, but it's not the same. It's like how I like Kip, which is nothing compared to how I like Bob (and Kip isn't coming back because Mrs. F said she's coming back to school on Monday!). So anyhow, after I came to Mrs. F's, Maxine showed up, then came Ann and then came Bev! We all had the same idea, which is so coolsville, if you ask me. And we confronted Mrs. F and came up with a plan. Then we sent James to go make up with Mary!

I have to catch some zzzz's Diary, I'll tell you the rest tomorrow!

Love,
Judy Jenkins

PS — don't worry, Bob is fine!
Thank goodness!

How can I expect to see world peace if I can't make peace with my own friends? So I did. I started with my own friends first.

I wonder when I wake up again, some-day perhaps soon, in 1955 if I will re-member any of this? It's a good thing I have this journal. And I'm keeping a copy of The Invisible Truth for proof, too!

Mrs. F. said we would go back eventu-ally. We couldn't get much more out of her, but it's better than nothing. I think...?

—Maxine

We're going to the quarterfinals!!! I had to pitch for Bob unexpectedly...he got his clock cleaned, but he'll be OK in time for next week's game. I struck out 4 hitters, a couple more popped up for easy outs; I allowed 2 runs, but got 3 RBIs. I laid out to catch a line drive up the middle and threw to second for a double play. And...Conrad Marshall? He saved me so I could save the game.

Dearest Irina,   22 May

I have finally done something noble in my short life. I have done what I have been expecting my friend Mary to do: put my friends first. I decided to sacrifice something (someone) and once I decided it, it was so easy to do...perhaps not a sacrifice, then? But I feel wonderful having done it and know it was the right thing to do. Whatever sadness I may feel is overshadowed by dignity and something else: is it freedom?

I look forward to hearing from you, my sweet cousin. I may just have to embrace "email" so that we can be in better touch.

Your Cousin Always,
   —Ann

PS It also helps to know that there are other fish in the sea, as they say. And some are just as cute and interesting!

After they had gone round and round, having agreed only on talking to James on Mary's behalf, it was Bev who had the solution.

"We can't just come right out and tell James that Mary likes him. We have to tell him that she needs his help. It's worked for . . . people I know."

Maxine smiled. Of course. She had given Bev this advice once upon a time.

"Oh, righto." Judy could see how this would work. "Now how do we get in touch with him?"

"I don't think it will be as hard as we think," Ann said, gesturing.

They were at the base of Mrs. F's staircase after having talked to her when James's car turned and pulled up the driveway. They waved hello and he got out of the car, approaching them cautiously.

"Good game, Beverly," he said, making conversation.

"Thanks."

"Maybe you can help us," Ann said.

"I guess I can try," he said, wary.

"Our friend, Mary, is feeling a little down and we don't know how to cheer her up," Maxine said.

"You see, her parents split up and she feels real terrible about it," Judy explained.

"And none of us quite know what to say to her, because we've never been in her shoes," said Ann. "None of us have parents who are divorced."

"She hasn't been acting like herself lately," Bev added pointedly. "She found out her dad's getting remarried. It's a real drag."

"You could just tell her that she's not alone . . . you know, be there for her," James offered.

"Yeah, we've tried that," Judy said.

"She just thinks we have it made in the shade and couldn't possibly understand," said Bev.

The girls waited patiently. Even Judy, who wanted to just ask James to go like Mary already. Instead, she said the thing that James wanted to hear: "We know you know about the whole, you know, time travel thing –"

"Judy!" Ann and Maxine gasped.

"*He knows,*" Judy insisted. To James, she said, "She needs your help. *We* need your help. We need our Mary back."

James was surprised to be having a conversation so openly about his theory; it wasn't lost on him that this was essentially an admission that his theory was correct. His heart started beating double-time.

"Well – I – of course I can help. Or I'd like to try . . . . "

The girls suggested that his first stop be Mary's.

He said he needed to check on Aunt Row and then he would go see Mary.

"I'm fine, Jimmy," said a voice from behind them.

They turned simultaneously to see Aunt Row leaning against a porch post comfortably, sipping an iced tea in the late evening. It was dusk, but they swore they saw her wink at them. And then she raised her glass.

"Hi, ladies. Didn't know you were here or I would have invited you in."

But they had a feeling that she did know that they were there and they would not have been surprised, seeing her there, if she had heard all of their conversation since they emerged from Mrs. F's apartment.

After James left, they walked home together, laughing and practically giddy. "That felt right," Ann said, and the others were relieved. "Friends forever." She smiled.

"Fifties Chix forever," Judy declared.

"That reminds me. Are you really going to start dressing like *that*?" Bev referenced Judy's clothes and the others chirped in. She just did not look like herself in a pair of skintight jeans and a glittered T-shirt that was cut too low.

Judy laughed. "No. I think I'll wear my poodle skirt on Monday. That'll really rattle Diane Dunkelman's cage."

They laughed again in agreement, looking forward to Monday, when Mrs. Fairview would be back in her place at the head of class. Maybe with James and Mary making up and Mrs. F back, they could go back to normal. Or at least a new normal.

"You're outside in the land of the living; I'll take that as a good sign," Row said to her friend. It was Sunday afternoon, the perfect time of day for lounging on the patio.

"Well, tomorrow's a work day, so I thought I'd better get some relaxing time in." May smiled. She was feeling better, as though the sun and fresh air were providing her with some clarity.

"I see you're doing some interesting reading." Row gestured to the newspaper titled *The Invisible Truth* lying on the table next to May's lemonade.

May adjusted her sunglasses. "I'd say 'interesting' is putting it mildly."

"When do you think they'll figure out who wrote that poem . . . and who it's about?"

"Right about when they realize Maxine's the one that wrote that essay called 'Useless Generation'."

"Tough times ahead," Row said. "They're going to need someone to lean on."

May sighed, shaking her head but smiling. Row was never subtle, even when she thought she was.

They heard movement in the driveway and saw James's car pull in.

Mary got out of the front seat, saying something to James, and then approached the ladies on the patio.

"Hi," she called, shielding her eyes from the sun. She must have just come back from church because she wore gloves and a hat with her light blue dress.

After a few pleasantries, she asked if she could talk to Mrs. F alone. Aunt Row obliged, going to check on her rose bushes.

Mrs. F fanned herself lightly with her big straw hat. "I thought I'd see you tomorrow at school," she said, but there was no edge in her voice.

"Oh, certainly. I just had to come by . . . I'm sorry to bother you on a Sunday . . . ." It felt silly to imply that they had a typical student-teacher relationship, but even with all that had happened, Mary respected the fact that Mrs. Fairview was first of all her social studies teacher and lastly . . . well, that remained to be seen.

"I had to return something to you." Mary pulled the Max Factor lipstick out of her pocket.

Mrs. F sat up. "You took this?"

"I was in your apartment when James was feeding Ike," Mary admitted. "I'm so sorry, I don't know why I took it. Except that . . . I have one just like it . . . and I thought it was some kind of sign."

Mrs. F seemed more relieved than angry. "I've kept it because it's my 'signature color'." She smiled. "This is the lipstick I wore when my husband proposed to me and the day I married him."

Mary was pleased at hearing this personal detail, no matter how minute. She wanted to ask May Fairview about her husband and why she wasn't with him, but instead offered a general "I'm sorry" once again.

"I guess it doesn't have to go on your permanent record," Mrs. F said playfully. She'd have to take the tube inside soon so it wouldn't melt, but in the meantime, she put it in a spot of shade in between her drink and *The Invisible Truth*.

"Oh," Mary said, noticing the paper. "Are you reading that?"

Mrs. F grabbed it up, more quickly than she meant to. "Sure. We try to stay on top of what the students are doing. Even the rabble-rousers."

"Well, I can't wait to read mine. But I haven't had time with the baby and all . . . . " It was the "and all" that really made it difficult, Mary added silently.

James waved from the car. "Hey, Mrs. F! Mary, Grace is crying."

Mary responded that she'd be there shortly. She and James were picking up the four other girls to go the fifties diner she had discovered the night before.

"Looks like you're figuring some things out," Mrs. Fairview murmured to Mary, gesturing towards James.

"I – I, uh . . . . " Mary blushed, worried that she was going against Mrs. F's wishes.

"It's not a criticism. I thought I was supposed to be the example for you, but it turns out you're teaching me a few things." Mrs. F decided on the spot that when Mary and James left, she would be calling her own dreamboat, Reggie. He'd said that when she was ready to come home, he'd be waiting.

Mary turned to go, but Mrs. F stopped her.

"Mary?" she said. "You should know that Mrs. Doss has had one extremely cranky baby every year that she's done this project. And she always gives the cranky one to her best student."

Mary threw her arms around Mrs. F. "Thank you, Mrs. Fairview. I'm actually going to miss this baby."

On Mary's way back to James, Mrs. F called after her, "You're finishing up the parenting project just in time to get the class assignment I give my class at the end of the year!"

Mary couldn't tell if her teacher was serious or joking. But she chose to take it as a joke. Because today she couldn't keep from smiling.

Dear Mrs. Doss,
This may not be the diary you had hoped for, but I can assure you that I learned a lot being a "mom" this past week. I named the baby Grace, which has turned out to be ironic because nothing about the experience has been particularly graceful! I did all the things I was supposed to do: bathe, feed, change and nurture the baby. That was hard enough. The real trick came when I had to keep living the rest of my life while maintaining Grace's. I learned a little more about being a mom, but I learned even more about being a friend, a daughter and a student. Grace taught me to never lose sight of those who love me; to fight hard, not for myself, but for my right to love them back. I am still mystified that a machine taught me all this! But there were lots of other things at play, including those friends and family that I mentioned, among other things. Having said all this, I hope you will enjoy my diary of this experience...and I hope my honesty about my frustration doesn't result in a lower grade!

Thank you for the opportunity.
Sincerely,
Mary J. Donovan
3rd Period

PS There's a rumor going around school that some of the "babies" are crankier than others. Do you know anything about that?

Epilogue

May's thoughts were fixated on how furious her mother would be. She sat in a grass-stained, torn wedding dress near a cliff on a grassy knoll in the middle of nowhere overlooking vast expanses of farmland and the Missouri River. After having abandoned her fiancé at the altar, here she was worried about her mother's feelings. There were far bigger things at stake . . . but she couldn't get past imagining the conversation with her mom that she knew was unavoidable.

The chauffeur was waiting with the car an acre or so back by the dirt road. After she had made him tear out of the church, he had asked – probably feeling foolish – "Where to?" She'd had him drive anywhere, just away, for a half hour or so until she'd told him to come here, the property Reggie had secured for the house they were going to build. It was forty minutes west of the city, perched high on top of a limestone bluff overlooking a fertile floodplain used for farming. The first time Reggie had taken her to see the place of their future estate, May had thought fancifully how the bluffs were a multi-layer cake and the soft grassy land on top was soft billowy frosting.

Her stomach tightened with guilt as she thought of the wedding cake she had left behind. She couldn't even see the view now without her glasses. Of course, she was really needing to see inwardly anyway. She rubbed her left wrist; it felt so empty without the gold watch, but she didn't want it today, and in fact hadn't been able to find it. Row had most likely hidden it so May couldn't obsess over it today. It was probably tucked in a box back at the apartment above Row's parents' garage, safe and sound, where it couldn't mess up anyone else's life.

"Miss Boggs, I presume?"

She jumped and caught her breath. Reggie had come up behind her. He held out her glasses and she gratefully received them and then looked back to see through a thicket of trees that there was a car behind the Roadmaster she had come in. She started to get up, but he put his hand gently on her shoulder. "No, no, I'll join you."

"Oh, Reggie –" she started. How could she ever tell him that what she had done had nothing to do with him? At least not in the way it might seem.

"May, if you don't mind, I'd like to bend your ear for a moment," he interrupted. He sounded so calm and easygoing. How was that possible? *May* wondered. And how did he know to find me here? And, most importantly, how did he still want to find me?

"I've had a good life, May, and I have nothing to complain about. But I've grown up doing exactly what everyone's expected of me. So, I decided when I found a gal I wanted to marry, it was to heck with everyone else. I found her, sweetheart; she's you. But I didn't stick to my guns. I know that wasn't the wedding you wanted back there . . . . " He paused, reached into his tuxedo for a cigarette, put it in his mouth, and looked thoughtfully at his bride. She was always pleading with him to quit smoking, because, he realized, she loved

him; and so he didn't light up. "I still want to marry you, Marion Boggs. I'm betting you ran away from all that because it's not you. You saw your future and you weren't even in it. Am I right?"

May's eyes teared up. It was exactly right. She nodded.

"Tell me, do you still want me in your future?"

She nodded again.

"I hoped that was what you'd say." He stood up and brushed himself off, then reached for her hand to help her stand with him. "May, will you still marry me . . . today?"

May glanced toward the cars and saw the minister, the chauffeur, and her beloved Rowena walking toward them. Row was carrying a Bible and a slightly wilted lily. Reggie took both of May's hands in his.

"Yes, oh, a thousand times yes!"

And so May did get to see Reggie become her husband that beautiful day in June in a torn, grass-stained bridal gown, on top of a wedding cake ridge, with her best friend Row at her side.

Marion dialed the number, her heart pounding as wildly as if it were her wedding day all over again. Thanks to modern technology, her groom knew she was calling him before he even heard her voice.

"Darling," he said with such kindness it took her breath away.

She faltered. "You lied to me. All this time, you knew."

"I could say the same."

She hadn't expected that. "Here it goes, then." She hoped the truth would make her free and hoped there would be enough room for freedom and love to coexist. "I will tell you something that I should have told you long ago. You were right about my gold watch, Reggie; it is special. I've been given a charge; for years I've wondered if it's a curse and for years I've assumed I needed to choose between you and my, uh, special projects associated with the watch."

"I know, May. I know everything. Just let me help you if that's what you need. Let me try. No more secrets."

"Tell me, do you still want me in your future?" she asked, repeating the question he'd asked her fifty-five years ago. Behind her, Ike declared "Reggie watch!" as if on cue.

"A thousand times yes," he said, and she could actually tell by his voice that he was smiling.

Ike was noticeably silent then and when she turned herself about in the kitchen, she found an empty perch next to the open window. Through the warm evening air, May could see Ike, already in the distance, soaring toward freedom, his red tail feathers streaking like a comet behind him. The breeze gently fluttered the lace curtains, exhaling in a fresh breath of hope.

May realized with a gasp that she and Ike were both free.

Glossary

Bad news: not good news! A person who is troublesome, undesirable, or unlikable

Beat: short for "beatnik"; hip and enlightened

Cloud nine: the best, your happy place

Cooties: imaginary cause of someone's being totally uncool

DDT: Drop Dead Twice . . . worse than drop dead!

Eyeball: to take a gander at, look at

Fream: a freak or misfit

Frosted: angry, miffed

Get out of Dodge: to get out of somewhere fast; reference to Dodge City, Kansas and the portrayal of the wild west in old Western movies

Go ape: to freak out (go bananas!)

Goof: a clown or a fool; someone who messes up a lot

Goopy: messy or messed up

Goner: someone who is real gone – totally in love or crazy (or both)

Great Depression: a period in world history of severe economic depression that started with the stock market crash on what is known as "Black Tuesday," October 29, 1929, and lasting into World War II. A quarter of the US population was unemployed and farmers as well as industrialists were hit hard. Everyone learned to economize, making the most out of very little. Things that were broken were not thrown out or traded in, they were fixed. Leftovers weren't tossed out or fed to the dog, they were reheated. Franklin D. Roosevelt was elected as President in 1933 and instituted many federal programs (called the New Deal) that created jobs and public works projects that helped America start to pull out of the financial crisis. Social Security came out of this era.

Kooky: crazy, nuts

Latkes: Jewish potato pancakes eaten especially during Hanukkah; the oil the pancakes are fried in is suggestive of the oil that lasted for eight days in the temple that Hanukkah commemorates

Mary's Macaroni and cheese (recipe): During the Great Depression, macaroni and cheese was a popular dish because it was cheap and tasty. By the 1950s, it was a staple in homes and cafeterias. Here is the recipe that Mary uses (adapted from her Nana's recipe):

Mary's macaroni and cheese (serves 6)

Ingredients:

2 cups dry macaroni, cooked until tender (better overcooked and soft than al dente) and drained

1 teaspoon of salt

2 cups cubed sharp cheddar cheese (sharp cheddar is best for taste)

1 teaspoon mustard powder

2 cans evaporated milk

1 cup Panko (bread) crumbs (Panko stays crispier)

Grease a casserole with butter and set it aside. Preheat oven to 350F. Put a layer of the macaroni in the pan and sprinkle with a layer of the cheese, then sprinkle with salt and mustard. Repeat layers, ending with macaroni. Sprinkle generously with pepper. Pour milk over all and sprinkle breadcrumbs on top. Bake for 30 minutes. Makes excellent leftovers!

Pad: house, home

Rattle one's cage: to get all out of sorts, disturbed, or upset

Royal shaft: a huge injustice

Sufganiyot: Jewish fried donuts eaten to celebrate Hanukkah

Sukkot: Jewish holiday that celebrates the fall festival and commemorates the Jews' wandering in the desert wilderness for forty years after Sinai. In Hebrew, "sukkot" means "booth" or "hut" and refers to the tabernacle. Often, huts are built in back-yards and lived in during the holiday in commemoration of the temporary dwellings the Children of Israel lived in during the forty years in the desert. The holiday is similar to Thanksgiving in many ways because the early American settlers looked to the Bible for how to give thanks for their survival and the harvest. See Leviticus 23:33.

The most: the coolest or best ever

Threads: clothes

van Gogh (1853-1890): a masterful post-impressionist French artist who was a failed and starving artist, having sold only two paintings (out of 2,000!) in his lifetime. However, in 1990, a century after his suicide, one of his paintings, *Portrait of Dr. Gachet,* sold for $82.5 million. It was one of the most expensive paintings ever sold.

BE KEPT IN ORBIT, HEP CATS!

Look for these other titles in the Fifties Chix series:

Book 1: Travel to Tomorrow

Book 3: Third Time's a Charm

Book 4: Broken Record

Book 5: Till the End of Time

Check out **www.FiftiesChix.com** and join the Fan Club for updates on the Fifties Chix book series, more info on your fave characters, secret diary entries, contests, and more!

Also visit the Fifties Chix wiki at

http://fiftieschix.wikispaces.com

for extended activities and fun educational stuff.

"Like" Fifties Chix on **Facebook**. And ... **"Friend" Judy E. White on Facebook! (She has her own page, remember?)**

BOOK 1

travel to
tomorrow

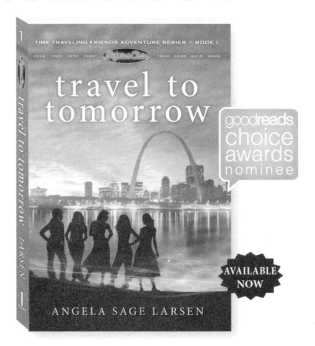

Sock hops. Soda fountains. Slumber parties. Life in 1955 is simple for tomboy Beverly, moody Maxine, high-spirited Judy, studious Mary and artistic Ann. But after a class assignment to predict life in the future, they wake up the next morning in a future they could never have imagined (having time-traveled into a parallel universe to the 21st century. With only each other to trust, they must work together and find their way "home" to 1955; but the more they discover about the future, will they even want to go back?

SIGN UP TO GET UPDATES AND READ SNEAK PREVIEWS OF UPCOMING BOOKS AT FIFTIESCHIX.COM

BOOK 3

third time's a charm

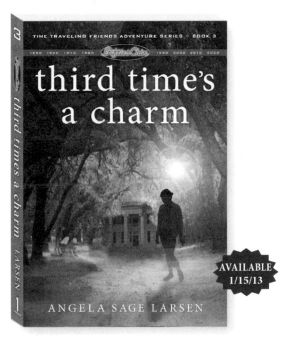

In 1945, May Boggs, the Fifties Chix' social studies teacher, is 15 years old. World War II has taken its toll and May and her two best friends, Rowena and Emily, are happy to see the war coming to an end at long last. But their bright futures are disrupted by a trip back to another war-torn era–the Civil War. When in modern day, Maxine pays the price for the controversial essay she wrote for the school's underground paper, the secret her teacher uncovers in 1865 may be the very thing that saves Maxine's–and the Fifties Chix' –reputation and future. Jump in and join the time-traveling adventures of three generations of friends who fight for freedom, friendship and their special place in the world in the third book of the Fifties Chix series.

SIGN UP TO GET UPDATES AND READ SNEAK PREVIEWS OF UPCOMING BOOKS AT FIFTIESCHIX.COM

Premiere
http://premiere.fastpencil.com